See You at
HARRY'S

JO KNOWLES

**WALKER
BOOKS**

The author gratefully acknowledges permission from
Merrit Malloy to quote from her poem "Epitaph"

First published in Great Britain 2013 by Walker Books Ltd
87 Vauxhall Walk, London SE11 5HJ

2 4 6 8 10 9 7 5 3 1

Text © 2012 Jo Knowles
Cover illustration © 2013 Walker Books Ltd

The right of Jo Knowles to be identified as author of
this work has been asserted by her in accordance with
the Copyright, Designs and Patents Act 1988

This book has been typeset in Sabon

Printed and bound in Great Britain by Clays Ltd, St Ives plc

British Library Cataloguing in Publication Data:
a catalogue record for this book is available from the British Library

ISBN 978-1-4063-4607-7

www.walker.co.uk

For Scott—

Thank you for being my
protector, dreamer, adventurer,
and sometimes partner in crime.
But mostly for being my brother
and all that means.

I miss you.

1

THE VERY BEST DAY OF MY LIFE, I threw up four times and had a fever of 103 degrees. I was pretty sure I was going to die, and sometimes by the look on my mom's face every time she took my temperature, I think she was pretty sure, too. It was all because of Random Smith, a boy in school who never had any lunch. I'd given him a bite of my sandwich and all of my crackers, he looked so hungry. Growing up, my mom wasn't the kind of mom who said never drink from the same cup as someone else. That stuff didn't occur to her. So I'd given him a sip of my milk, too.

But in addition to being hungry all the time, Random was also usually sick. People never knew what he had, so they always just said he had "some random thing"—which they all thought was hilarious but I just thought was mean.

That day at home, my mom spent every minute with me. My older sister and brother were at school, and my dad was working at my parents' restaurant. I was eight and had never been home alone with just my mom before, at least not all day and definitely not with her full attention. The house was so quiet, except for us two. My mom got into bed with me and read *Charlotte's Web*. It took all day, and at the end, we both cried and shared a tissue.

When we finished sniffling, my mom adjusted herself in the bed so she could look at me. "Fern," she said softly. "Do you know why I named you Fern?"

I nodded, looking at the drawing of the girl on the cover of the book.

"Why?" she asked.

"Because Fern is one of your favourite characters?"

"And why is that?"

I shrugged.

"Because Fern cares," she said. "From the moment you were born, I could tell you had a special soul.

8

I knew you'd be a good friend. A hero."

I looked at my chest and tried to feel my soul buried in there, deep in my heart.

"It's true," my mom said. "Not everyone would share a sandwich with Random Smith."

I smiled, feeling my soul stir a little.

My mom took my hand and kissed it. "I'm proud of you, honey," she said. "I know you're miserable now, but you made a little boy feel like he matters. And I hope you think it was worth all this."

I nodded slowly, thinking about Random and his dirty face and stinky unwashed hair. I wondered if he was home sick, too, and if he had a mom next to him on his bed, reading to him all day and telling him he was special. But then I started to feel like I was going to throw up again. So I turned over on my side and my mother rubbed my back in slow, tiny circles, humming a lullaby I barely remembered, with fingers on my back I hardly knew. She was always so busy cooking and cleaning and working at the restaurant and basically just taking care of everything else.

I closed my eyes and tried to remember that feeling, because somehow, even then, I had a hunch that I might not feel it again.

Two days later, my mom got Random's bug. But instead of getting better, she kept throwing up. Every morning she was sick, sick, sick. And then finally, after what felt like weeks and weeks, she and my dad sat us all down and told us the news. My mom was going to have a baby. Now Charlie sits in the back of my mom's station wagon between Holden and me. He's three years old and thinks no one's looking when he picks his nose, which is way too often. My mom and sister are in the front, arguing about how many hours my sister has to work at the restaurant to help "contribute" to the family. Since Sara couldn't get into any good colleges, she's doing a gap year by staying at home and working at my parents' restaurant. All her friends went off to college, so on top of everything else, she's lonely and grumpy and not much fun to be around.

"Tell me again why you're dragging us to the restaurant, Mom," Holden says, leaning as far away from Charlie as he can in case he decides to fling one of his finds in Holden's direction.

"I told you it's a surprise," my mom answers.

"Yay!" Charlie reaches for my ear. He loves playing with people's ears when he's not picking his nose or talking to Doll, the plastic baby he found in the memory trunk in my closet, where I put all my old toys and which was supposed to be private.

"Stop it," I mutter, flicking his sticky hand away.

Doll sits on his lap, facing forward, her naked bottom balanced on his knees.

"You need to put some clothes on her," I tell him.

He giggles and makes her dance naked in the air.

When my parents told us my mom was having a baby, they said we kids could pick a name together. My favourite book at the time was *Charlie and the Chocolate Factory*. We all agreed that if we had to have a new brother, one like Charlie would be OK. We thought he'd be destined to be the kind of kid who'd get picked to ride in the great glass elevator. The sweet kid. The smart kid. The *quiet* kid. So far, it seemed like our Charlie wasn't quite filling the bill.

"Mom?" Holden asks again. "Is this a *Dad* surprise?"

"It better not be," Sara answers. She fidgets with her dreadlocks and flips down the sun visor so she can look at herself in the mirror. Sara's trying to be a Dead Head, like my parents were before they had us kids. Only the Grateful Dead doesn't even exist anymore, so I don't know what that's all about.

"I don't know exactly what your father has planned,"

my mom says. "But please, kids, try to humour him, OK?"

Humouring my dad means humiliation for us.

The last time my dad had a surprise, it involved the most embarrassing family/business Christmas card in history. My dad and mom dressed up as Santa and Mrs. Claus, and Holden, Sara, and I were forced to be elves. Charlie was Rudolph, but he kept pulling off his red nose so he could pick at the real one underneath it.

Charlie reaches for my ear again.

"Stop it!" I yell.

"Fern, please. He only does it because he loves you," my mom says.

"I love you, Ferny," Charlie says in his extra-baby voice.

"Whatever," I say, looking out the window.

"Whatevuh," Charlie repeats.

"Please don't teach him that, Fern. It's bad enough coming from you."

I sigh and stare out the window. I can feel Charlie reaching Doll out to dance at me, but I ignore him.

"Whatevuh," he makes Doll whisper in my ear. Charlie has trouble pronouncing his *r*'s except when he says my name. My mom says this is the greatest compliment Charlie could possibly give, working so hard to say my name correctly. I guess it's true, but Charlie is so annoying so often, it's hard to feel flattered.

"I just want you to know," Holden says to my mom, "if this has anything to do with the annual Christmas card, I'm telling you right now, there is no way I'm wearing elf ears again."

Charlie pulls Doll away from me and reaches for Holden's ear.

"Listen," my mom says, all serious. "I'm sure whatever your dad has planned will be fine. He loves you. He's just trying to do what he thinks is best for the business."

"What about what's best for us?" Sara asks.

"It's all the same. If the business does well, then we do well," my mom says, quoting one of my dad's familiar lines.

Sara crosses her arms. "Whatever," she says.

My mom just sighs, and we continue to drive in silence, except for Charlie's quiet singing of "Rudolph, the Red-Nosed Reindeer" in Doll's left ear. I lean my head against the window and watch the neighborhood houses swim by, wondering if all families are as frustrating to live with as mine.

2

WHEN WE GET TO THE RESTAURANT, my dad
hurries over to us with a huge grin on his face. "Finally!
What took you so long? The photographer will be here
any minute. Quick, kids, put these on."

We're still in the parking lot as he hands us each a
neon-coloured T-shirt. I notice that he's careful not to
unfold them so that we can't see the drawing on the
front. I don't know why, since he's sporting his own
neon-yellow T. As soon as he hands out all the shirts,
his chest is in full view and so is the horrible design –
a huge dinosaur sitting on top of a badly drawn image

14

of our restaurant. The dinosaur is eating an ice-cream cone, and drips are slipping down the front window. Little faces peek out the window around the drips. I think they are supposed to be ours.

"You've got to be kidding me," Sara says. "Seriously, Dad?"

My mom gives her a warning look.

"What?" my dad asks as he helps Charlie pull an electric-blue shirt over his head.

"We *all* have dinosaurs?" I ask.

"What's wrong with dinosaurs? Kids love 'em. Right, Charlie?"

Charlie nods excitedly and roars.

"What do dinosaurs have to do with Christmas?" I ask. "These are for the annual card, right?"

"Come on, come on, come on. We don't have time for dillydallying," my dad says, ignoring my question.

I pull my own bright orange T over my head. It feels bulky over the T-shirt I'm already wearing. Sara puts hers on inside out. My dad is so busy fussing with Charlie, he doesn't even notice.

"I can't believe we have to do this," Holden says, stretching his neon-green T-shirt out in front of him. "And why did I have to get green? It makes me look pale."

My mom clears her throat in this way she has that means we're supposed to look over at her without making it obvious. We all look and watch as her right hand, which is in a fist, slowly unclenches and she stretches out five fingers.

Holden, Sara, and I exchange glances. We wait.

My mom sighs and slowly unclenches her other fist. Five more fingers. That's ten bucks each if we keep our mouths shut and cooperate.

We're in.

I don't know when my mom turned to silent bribery to prevent family conflicts, but it seems to work. It's not that we want to disappoint my dad. We know he means well. But why do his ideas always have to be so lame and humiliating? And why does the humiliating part always have to include us?

We all follow my dad to the front of the restaurant, where he starts to position us under the window just as a van pulls into the parking lot blasting the Grateful Dead. It's "Uncle John's Band," Charlie's favourite, and he immediately starts shaking his bum.

"They're here!" my dad yells.

Sara fidgets with her dreadlocks again. "At least they have good taste in music."

"Everyone, this is Eric," my dad says when the photographer walks over to us. "And Sky," he says, gesturing to a woman wearing a head scarf.

"I love your hair," Sky says to Sara.

"Uh, that's not a regular camera," Holden points out when Eric lifts the camera to his shoulder.

"That's the surprise!" my dad yells. "Surprise! We're making a commercial! Isn't that great?"

"Yay!" Charlie yells, and runs over to hug Eric's legs.

We all look at my mom. "Um, wow, honey!" she says. "I had no idea!" She makes an apologetic face at us, but she knows very well there is no amount of money that is going to make us be OK with *this* plan.

"That's why it's a *surprise*!" my dad says. He's beaming, as if this is the best idea he has ever had. "OK, OK. Let's get set up." He puts his hands on my shoulders and walks me backward so I'm standing under the huge sign in front of the restaurant. "You look terrific, sweetheart!" he says in my ear. His stale coffee breath is particularly pungent.

"Holden? You next. Right here beside Ferny."

"I want Ferny!" Charlie whines. He grabs hold of my legs so tightly, I almost fall over.

"Watch it!" I yell. "And don't call me Ferny!" I hate that name.

"Daddy said it first!"

"You're not Dad!"

"Stop it, Fern," my mom says. "He's paying you a compliment." Any time Charlie bugs me and I complain about it, my mom tells me I should be flattered. Flattered because he's the only one in this family who ever pays any attention to me? I don't think she gets how insulting that is.

My dad continues to line us up so that finally Sara, Holden, and I are squeezed in between my mom and dad. My dad picks up Charlie and perches him on his shoulder.

"I'm not doing this," Sara says, stepping out of line.

"Now, look, honey," my dad says. "I'm paying these people a lot of money. And with any luck, we'll get it back tenfold when the business starts booming."

"I don't want business to boom. That's just more work for me."

"More *money* for you, sweetheart," my dad says through gritted teeth. "You want your own car to take with you to college next year?"

My sister perks right up. "Seriously?"

My dad nods. "Now try to look happy."

Sara gets back in line, and we all plaster on our happy faces.

"Just try to act normal," Eric says, fiddling with the camera lens.

"That'll be a first," Holden mumbles.

"That's us, one big normal family," I whisper back.

"Hush, you two," my mom hisses.

"Harry, you ready?"

We all look at my dad. His name is George.

"Ready when you are!" my dad says.

Eric holds up his hand and counts silently on his fingers. Five, four, three, two, one, then points to my dad.

"WELCOME TO HARRY'S!" my dad booms.

Holden's sweaty arm rubs against mine. My mom is stiff behind me. I hope the camera is zoomed in on my dad because I think I cringed when he started talking. I try to smile as he lists off the most popular flavors of ice cream we sell.

"...and our most popular, Dinosaur *Crunch*!"

I hear Charlie chomp like a dinosaur. My dad laughs way too loud, then clears his throat. "IF YOU HAVEN'T BEEN TO HARRY'S, YOU HAVEN'T BEEN TO HEAVEN!" he yells.

Sky motions for all of us to wave. Charlie flaps his arm frantically and shouts, "See you at Hawee's!" in his worst baby voice yet.

I think my ears are bleeding.

"Aaaaand cut," Eric says.

My dad tosses Charlie in the air. "Great line, buddy!" he yells. "Should we do another take, Eric? I'm not sure how that came out."

"Nah, Harry. It was perfect. We'll cut anything that doesn't look quite right and pan in on some scenes I'll take inside. I'd like to film some customers eating cones, sundaes – stuff like that."

"Sure, sure, sure," my dad says. "Right this way." We all follow him into the restaurant, which is half empty. Right away I can tell my dad has planted "customers"—our regular employees and their kids or little sisters and brothers. They all say hi to my dad like he's a local hero, though I notice none of them call him by his real name.

My dad never corrects people when they call him Harry. He says it's good for business because people like to think they're talking to the guy the restaurant is named after (who was actually my grandfather). I'm pretty sure this drives my mom a little nuts, but she doesn't say anything. My mom almost never yells or gets upset. Whenever she looks like she might start to lose it, she heads up to my dad's stuffy office and shuts the door so she can meditate. There's a sign on the door that she flips around before she closes and locks it. On one side, it says, *Please knock.* On the other, it says, *Mom is finding her inner peace. Come back later.* I'm not really sure what would happen if we interrupted her during meditation, and I don't really want to find out.

Charlie follows Eric around for the next hour while he films people eating burgers and licking ice-cream cones. Sara, Holden, and I sit at one of the booths.

"I can't believe this," Sara says for like the hundredth time as we watch the film crew. "Thank God I'm out of high school. I would never live this one down."

"Oh, thanks a lot," Holden says. "I'm just *starting*! I have enough stacked against me already. Now this?"

"What do you mean?" I ask.

"Just forget it."

But I think I know.

I lean back in the booth and sigh. "We're doomed," I say.

Sara shakes her head. She doesn't even bother to try to cheer us up because she knows we're right.

The bell on the front door tinkles, and Random Smith walks in. He's wearing a T-shirt that says GLOW on it, and I wonder what it's supposed to mean. Ran is always wearing T-shirts with sayings on them that don't quite make sense to me. Last year, he gave me one for my birthday that said REAL. I think he was upset that I never wore it. I smile at him as he comes up to the table and waves the way he always does – elbow at his waist, hand swishing back and forth like a windshield wiper. Like a robot.

"Hey, Fern," he says.

"Hey, Ran." When I slide over, the back of my thighs stick to the red vinyl seat and make a disgusting sound. Honestly, could my life get any more embarrassing?

A few things about Ran have changed since our days of swapping germs:

1. His mom, who was really sick from cancer back then, won her battle, and she and Ran's dad started an online T-shirt company that makes a ton of money.

2. Ran shaved his head when his mom lost all her hair from chemotherapy, and he just decided he liked being bald. So now his head

is shaved really close. I don't think most people could pull this off, but Ran is a very no-nonsense kind of person, and he doesn't really care what other people think. Also, it actually looks pretty good.

3. Despite his weirdness, Ran became my best friend. With his mom all better, he also stopped being so messy and sick all the time, which is a good thing, because being his best friend meant I was sick almost just as much.

Sara winks at me and I blush.

"What's going on?" Ran asks, taking in the scene.

"My dad is ending our lives as we know it," I say.

"TV commercial," Holden explains.

Ran cringes just as Charlie comes racing across the room and hugs him.

"Hey, little man," Ran says. They do their special handshake, which involves rubbing palms together. I don't think Ran knows or else cares how risky it is to touch Charlie's hands. No one knows where they've been – but most likely in some pretty disgusting places.

"Wanna sundae?" Charlie asks.

"Yeah!" Ran follows Charlie to the ice-cream counter, and they disappear behind it. A few minutes later, they return with a huge banana-split bowl filled with every topping we sell. They each have a spoon but share the bowl.

"That's disgusting," Sara says.

Charlie and Ran ignore her and go to town. Miraculously, they eat the whole thing. When they finish, Charlie's mouth has an almost-perfect chocolate circle around it that slowly drips down his chin. He looks just like the dinosaur on his T-shirt.

Ran carefully wipes his mouth with a napkin from the dispenser on the table. Then, instead of getting a new one, he just folds it over and wipes Charlie's mouth for him. Charlie beams.

In the distance, my dad tries to get the line cooks behind the counter to say, "See you at Harry's," but they look kind of confused. Instead, Charlie yells it from our table.

I hide my face in my hands.

"What's wrong?" Ran asks with his familiar bewildered look.

"Can't you tell how lame this commercial is going to be?" I ask him.

"Well, yes," he says slowly. "But that's not *your* fault."

"Since when does it matter if an embarrassing moment is your fault or not?" I ask him. "Do you not remember the elf cards? It took months for me to live that down."

"Only because you let it bother you," he says calmly.

"Whatever," I say, staring at the orange letters on his T-shirt. GLOW. Yeah. Why is it so easy for Ran to just glow, when I'm the one wearing the neon T-shirt?

3

"LET'S GET OUT OF HERE," Sara says when we finally can't listen to my dad anymore. "Ran? You need a ride home?"

"I have my bike," he says. "Thanks for the ice cream, little man." He does his handshake with Charlie again. This time their hands sort of stick, and Ran has to wipe his on his jeans.

"See you later, Fern." He gives me an odd salute before he turns to leave.

In the car, Holden turns around from the front seat and grins at me. "So, Fern. What's with Random, huh?"

"What do you mean?"

"Ran? He's looking pretty cute these days."

Sara eyes me in the rearview mirror. "Yeah, Fern. What's up with that?"

"Um, I don't control people's metamorphoses."

Charlie makes Doll look at me with her unchanging surprised expression.

"Where'd you learn *that* word?" Holden asks.

I shrug.

"So, anyway, are you two going to be more than just friends? I could see him looking at you in that special way." Holden raises his eyebrows.

"Random and Ferny sitting in a tree…" Sara sings.

Charlie makes Doll dance.

"I think it's time for all of you to shut up now," I say.

"Bad word!" Charlie says, hitting me with Doll's head.

"Ow! Knock it off." I push Doll away and look out the window.

The truth is, I don't really know how I feel about Ran. When he smiles at me as if I am more than his childhood best friend, sometimes it makes me happy. Sometimes it makes me scared.

"If you don't snatch him up, someone else will," Holden says.

"Like you, Mr. Faggypants?" Sara reaches over to pinch Holden's cheek. "Better watch out, Fern."

Holden hits Sara's hand away. But she just laughs. "Chill out – I'm only joking."

"I can't believe you," he says, turning away from her to glare out the window.

"You people need to lighten up," Sara says.

At the stop sign just before the turn to our house, Holden jumps out of the car, slams the door, and starts walking.

"Oh, please," Sara says. "No one can take a joke."

"Your jokes aren't funny," I say. "You hurt his feelings."

"Well, he better grow a thicker skin soon if he's going to survive high school."

"Why?"

"Because he wears who he is on his impeccably ironed J.Crew sleeve – that's why. I mean, he's like the quintessential fag."

"What's a fag?" Charlie asks.

"A boy who likes boys instead of girls," Sara says.

"And it has nothing to do with how someone dresses!" I yell.

"Except in Holden's case," Sara says calmly.

"I know you think you're funny, but you're not. And stop saying that word!"

"Just telling it like it is, Ferny."

I wish Sara could be more like the Sara she was named after from *A Little Princess*. That Sara is nice to everyone. Even the mice in the attic. This Sara seems to find it necessary to look for everyone's weak spot. And then stomp on it.

When we get home, Charlie runs around the yard with Doll, throwing her in the air, then catching her and kissing her.

An hour or so later, my dad drops my mom off. He's all excited about taking the delivery truck someplace for another surprise. My mom gives me and Sara a look that tells us to zip it, but even she seems pretty wary.

"Holden ran away!" Charlie says as my dad pulls back out of the driveway.

"*What?*" my mom asks, dropping a bag of groceries. "Where did he go?"

"Faggypants, faggypants," Charlie sings, walking

around my mom in a circle as he traces his finger across her legs.

"Stop it, Charlie. That's not nice." She looks at me and Sara accusingly. "And who taught him that lovely word?"

I can't believe she has to ask.

"I was only joking around," Sara says.

"Which way did he go?"

"He got out at the stop sign on the corner," I say.

"Sara, take Charlie inside and give him a snack. Fern, go find your brother, would you, hon? You're the only one who seems to be able to bring him back."

Holden is always running off in a huff, and I am always the one searching for him and bringing him home. Holden's named after the main character in *The Catcher in the Rye*. I wasn't supposed to read it until I'm older, but I snuck my mom's paperback copy out of her room last year. The pages were all soft from her reading it so many times. The book is about this boy who's depressed because he thinks everyone he knows is a phony, so he runs away. I understand why my mom likes the book and all, but I personally think it was a big mistake to name your kid after a boy who tries to kill himself, even if he is thoughtful and brilliant. My favourite parts in the book are when the main character talks about his little sister, Phoebe. Sometimes I think I'm a little like Phoebe to our Holden. Because in the book she's the one he goes back for. And that's sort of like me. Only I have to go looking for him first.

I find Holden sitting under the huge pine tree in our next-door neighbor's yard. They're never home, so it's a good hideout. He showed it to me when Charlie was born and I used to get upset and jealous. I felt like I went from being a shadow to being completely invisible. Holden told me the tree cave would always be our special place that no one else in our family would know about.

"Knock, knock," I say, standing just outside.

"Who's there?" Holden asks.

"Boo."

"Boo who?"

"Don't cry." I bend low under the bottom boughs and crawl under. It's cool and smells like Christmas.

"I don't know why you bother coming after me," he says, picking at the rubber on the sole of his sneakers the way he always does.

"I'm your sister. That's my job."

"And Mom sent you."

"I would've come anyway."

He buries a piece of shoe rubber under some brown dried-up needles.

"So, you coming home soon?" I ask.

"I dunno. I kind of like it under here. It needs some decorating, but..."

"Holden? Is it true, what Sara said?"

"That I'm too sensitive? No."

I nudge him. "Come on, you know what I'm talking about."

"Yeah, I know."

I wait for him to really answer, but he doesn't. He just sits there with his arms crossed over his knees. If it's true, I wonder what that must be like. To know you're different. To know some people are going to hate you because of it.

We're quiet under the pine, smelling Christmas in summer and listening to the traffic on our street pick up as people start getting home from work. It's my favourite thing about Holden, being able to sit quietly together and not talk. Just think together and not have to say a single word. But today, for the first time, I feel something floating between us, a question I'm sure I know the answer to. I feel the weight of the answer separating us for some reason I don't understand. If it doesn't matter to me, why should it matter to him?

"I don't care if what Sara said is true," I tell him quietly, hoping my words will make the floating thing go away.

He takes a deep breath that sounds like it hurts. I wait for him to say something, but he just sits there, staring at the pine needles. And it almost feels like the floating thing has swallowed him up, leaving me all alone.

4

ABOUT A WEEK LATER, my dad waves a puffy manila envelope at us and calls a mandatory family and staff meeting at the restaurant. He rounds us all up in his office. It's the hottest day of the summer, I think. August. And the office is packed with our family, the wait staff, the cook, and the line crew. We're all crammed into the tiny room in the attic among cardboard boxes, paper products, and my mom's meditation stuff. A dusty old fan buzzes hot air at us from the one window in the room. Instead of cooling anyone off, it just blows the stinky mixture of body odor, kitchen grease, and my dad's coffee breath. I think I'm going to throw up.

My dad opens his laptop and holds up a disc that he handles as if it could crack at any moment. "Just arrived today!" he says, smiling like a maniac. "I haven't even viewed it myself!"

My mom makes a tiny noise. I think it's actually a whimper. One of the new cooks is standing on her meditation cushion. She closes her eyes, and I can tell she's taking a deep breath. I am pretty sure she's going to have a hard time finding her inner peace any time soon.

Charlie claps his hands.

I breathe through my mouth to keep from gagging on the growing smell.

"Here we go, here we go," my dad says quietly as he slips the disc into the computer.

"Go, go, go!" Charlie yells. He hugs my dad's knee.

An image of the Harry's sign on top of the restaurant comes into view, then the camera pans lower to show us all standing there.

"Woo-hoo!" someone in the back of the room yells.

Holden moans.

"Shhh," my dad says, and the room gets quiet.

On the screen, my dad is listing all the ice-cream

flavors we sell at Harry's. The camera zooms in on our faces. Charlie is inspecting my dad's ear as he talks. I see myself cringe in the corner of the screen and feel myself do it again. There are a few shots of inside the restaurant while my dad's voice-over talks about how great it is to be running a second-generation business and how he's made every attempt to preserve the authentic feel of the place. I glance over at my mom, who shows no expression at all. Sara told me that when my dad inherited the restaurant, my mom wanted to renovate the place and sell organic vegetarian dishes, but my dad said the business would never survive and that he couldn't bring himself to destroy his own dad's dreams of making Harry's truly famous one day. I guess my mom must have thought that was a noble-enough reason because whenever my dad comes up with these business schemes, my mom is always at his side.

"There's Mona! There's Patrick!" the staff shout as the camera pans to various staff members.

"Shhh," Charlie says with his wet finger to his lips.

I see Ran with Charlie behind the counter, holding up the sundae they made. My stomach flutters when Ran smiles at the camera, and I feel myself blush. I look around, as if anyone could actually tell what just happened. But Holden nudges me and winks, and I realize maybe someone can.

The scene flicks back to our family standing in front of the sign and my dad mentioning heaven. Then it zooms right into Charlie's dirty angel face when he says, "See you at Hawee's!" at the top of his lungs.

The screen goes black, and then the store hours appear in neon-green text.

There are cheers, but I barely hear them. I am already imagining how this will play out at school. It is not a good scenario.

"Well?" my father asks, turning in his swivel chair to face us.

"Again!" Charlie cheers, pointing to the screen.

My dad tousles his hair.

"Born actor!" someone says.

Holden snorts.

"Fern, honey, remind me that we have to contact Ran's parents and get them to sign a release form so he can be in the ad. I'd hate to cut that scene. It's nice to have some diversity."

"Di-what?" Charlie asks.

I roll my eyes. "It means Dad wants to use Ran because he has darker skin than the rest of us."

"Oh, Ferny," my dad says, tucking in his enormous T-shirt where it keeps coming untucked because it's too small and only emphasizes how huge his belly has gotten. "I'm not *using* him. It's just a nice coincidence. Just like Mona."

Oh, my God. I can't believe he just said that. Mona, who is Chinese American, is a waitress who has worked at the restaurant for a million years and used to babysit us all the time, too. She just shrugs. Everyone always just shrugs when my dad says something stupid. *He means well,* my mom always says. Whatever.

"So," he says to everyone else, "the first ad will air at the end of the month! Just in time for the fall tourists. Just you wait. Just you wait! They'll be flowing through the doors."

A quiet, sarcastic *great* sweeps through the stifling room. My dad seems to be the only one interested in increasing business at Harry's. I think everyone else just sees a busier restaurant as more work. Most of the people who work here are what my mom calls strays. People who are down on their luck. People she thinks she can help save. I think it's the only part about owning the restaurant that she really likes – being able to help give people jobs, even though waiting and bussing tables is hardly a good time.

"Well, back to work, work, work!" my dad says cheerfully.

A few people roll their eyes behind his back. I see my mom notice and cringe. My poor dad. The thing is he really does mean well. He's just … a little intense. Sometimes I look at the old photo albums my mom keeps to see that he wasn't always like he is now, so obsessed with the business and making it busier. My sister loves to tell the story of how before they had us kids, my parents followed the Grateful Dead on tour and camped out in people's fields and stuff. But then my grandparents died, and my dad inherited the business. And soon after that, my mom got pregnant. I think Sara is secretly devastated that Jerry Garcia, the lead singer, died, because she is obsessed with their music, and I'm sure she would love to camp out in strangers' fields, too. But I just like hearing the stories and looking at the pictures because my parents look so happy and relaxed in them. And it makes me think that if they could be that way once, maybe someday they will be again.

5

A FEW DAYS LATER, we're in the kitchen helping my mom with dinner when the phone rings. When my mom hangs up, she tells us that we have to go out to the driveway for some sort of surprise from my dad.

"What now?" Holden asks.

"I'm sure it's not that bad," my mom says.

Sara and I sigh at the same time.

"Why do you guys always have to assume the worst?" my mom asks.

"Do you really have to ask?"

"Oh, Fern, don't be so negative."

"Should we all put our T-shirts on in case the camera crew is coming to the house?" Sara asks.

Charlie, who is already wearing his, pats the dinosaur on his tummy.

"Let's just get outside," my mom says.

We all follow her out to the driveway. Charlie takes my hand and swings it back and forth. Even though his hand is sticky, it feels kind of nice that he picked my hand to take instead of my mom's or Sara's. He looks up at me and smiles. "I like supwises."

"Not this kind," Holden mumbles.

Charlie frowns. I squeeze his hand to reassure him, even though I have to agree with Holden.

In the distance, we hear the familiar roar of the ice-cream truck.

"Daddy!" Charlie yells. He lets go of my hand and starts to run down the driveway.

"Charlie, get back here!" My mom runs after him and pulls him onto the grass.

My dad honks the horn and swings the truck into the driveway.

"Oh. My. God," Sara says.

I stare at the side of the truck with my mouth open. My mom drags Charlie back up the driveway but stops halfway and turns when she sees the looks on our faces. Charlie wriggles out of her grip and runs back to me as my dad comes around to us from the other side of the truck, beaming.

We all stand beside the truck and stare. Even Charlie is speechless.

"Well?" my dad finally asks. He's smiling bigger than I think I've ever seen. "Whaddaya think?"

The ice-cream truck used to say *Harry's Homemade Ice Cream and Family Restaurant* on it in fancy scrolled letters. Now the words are gone, and instead there is a giant photo of Charlie's face. He's licking an ice-cream cone in his dinosaur T-shirt. The front of it is covered with blue ice-cream drips and so is his chin. His long curls hang in his face so he looks like a girl. To the right of his face, there's a giant cartoon speech bubble that says in enormous letters SEE YOU AT HAWEE'S! Yes, it's spelled that way.

No one says a word.

My dad steps over to the truck and pats Charlie's enormous face. "Well, gang? Pretty great, huh?"

Charlie steps closer to the truck to get a better look. He blows a raspberry at his face, then turns around and shakes his bottom at it. I don't know what that means, but if I had to guess, it's Charlie's way of saying he looks ridiculous.

My dad ruffles Charlie's hair. "How's it feel to be famous, kiddo?"

Charlie head-butts my dad's leg.

"Wow, honey," my mom finally says.

Wow, honey could mean so many things. My mom has become an expert at using phrases this way. In her head, *Wow, honey* could mean:

1. "That is the craziest most ridiculous thing I have ever seen in my life! But I won't say so out loud because I don't want to upset you!" *or*

2. "How wonderful! Our child's face is on the side of a truck and now every looney-tunes pervert will know what he looks like! But I won't say so out loud because I don't want to upset you!" *or*

3. "Gee, I really thought I'd seen the worst of your ideas, but you continue to blow my mind by outdoing yourself! But I won't say so out loud because I don't want to upset you!"

But in my dad's head, it probably just means, "Wow. Exciting!"

So my mom gets to be sort of honest, and they don't get in a fight.

"It's all about brand recognition," my dad explains. "Everyone will love the commercial, but it's Charlie they'll remember. We've got to help them make the connection."

Holden and I swap looks. Charlie is a brand? The thought of my little brother's face riding through town every day with that stupid speech bubble makes me feel sick to my stomach.

I guess my dad was right about *brand recognition* because within a week of the ad coming out and the truck being on the road, people start recognizing Charlie at the restaurant.

"Look! It's that cute little girl on TV!" people say when they see him.

My dad never corrects them. Charlie doesn't, either. He just giggles and blows raspberries at them. And if the person is really excited, he does the bottom shake, too. While I admit this is kind of hilarious, it's also a little weird and embarrassing. Ran says this is what makes Charlie so cool. Because Charlie accepts who he is and doesn't care about *gender* issues.

I point out to Ran that Charlie is only three and doesn't even know what *gender* is.

"That's what I mean," Ran tells me.

Did I miss something?

No one besides my dad would have expected that an ad with a sweaty fat man and his awkward-looking family waving under a big sign could draw such a crowd, but that's what happens. They come in and beg Charlie to "say it." But Charlie always refuses.

"He's shy," my dad explains, leading them over to the ice-cream counter and encouraging them to try the "Super Smacker Sundae," which is the most expensive item on the ice-cream menu.

When my dad suggests printing up T-shirts with the Charlie image from the truck, my mom finally puts her foot down. "I don't want strangers wearing his face on their chests," she says. And even my dad has to admit when you put it like that, it's kind of creepy.

But business keeps picking up anyway. My dad buys more spots for the ad, and pretty soon all we have to do is turn on the TV and when the commercial breaks come on, so do we. My friend Cassie tells me someone even put it on YouTube. We suspect my dad, but when we grill him, he acts all innocent and says, "What's YouTube?" But the comments, which are all things like "Ben & Gary's can't hold a candle to Harry's!" pretty much give him away. My dad refuses to get their names right. Sometimes he refuses to say Jerry. Or sometimes he refuses to say Ben. But he never says both their correct names together. I think it really kills him that they have such a cool company, with tie-dyed T-shirts and stuff that is so much a part of what my parents *used* to be, what my mom *wanted* them to be. Instead, we sell lame dinosaur T-shirts. My dad would never admit this, of course. But I can tell.

Every time I see the commercial, I'm horrified at the sight of us in our pathetic T-shirts. My dad has no sense of style. The only one who looks remotely cool is Holden, who somehow manages to appear calm and oddly above the T-shirt he's wearing. I swear, Holden could be a model. Only in our town, people don't become models. In our town, the closest you get to fame is being on local TV with your family wearing ugly T-shirts while your dad sweats and your mom smiles in a strangely vacant way as if she had to go somewhere else in her mind just to get through the moment. And then your three-year-old brother says, "See you at Hawee's" in the most obnoxious voice known to mankind.

And that is definitely *not* the kind of fame you want.

Ever.

6

ON THE FIRST DAY OF SCHOOL, Holden and I wait for the bus together. I'm so nervous that I keep swallowing in an attempt to avoid throwing up. I wish Ran were here waiting with us. He never worries about stuff like the first day of middle school. He'll probably wear his black T-shirt that says CHILL in electric-blue letters.

My stomach twists. *Chill,* I tell it.

Holden stands on the edge of the road at the end of our driveway, finding stones to kick across the street. He's good at it. He has this way of stomping down at the edge of a stone and sending it flying all the way across. I stand next to him and give it a try, but I end up stomping on the stone and hurting the bottom of my foot.

"That's just sad," Holden says to me, then kicks another one.

This is the first time Holden and I have ever taken the bus together. Middle-school students and high-school students share buses because both schools are in one big building – middle school on the first floor, high school on the second.

We hear a truck engine, and he stops kicking and looks up the road. "God, I hate the bus," he says. "I can't believe we have to take it."

"What's so bad about the bus?" I ask.

He shakes his head and looks for another rock. "Bunch of losers," he mumbles.

Sometimes I think Holden imagines a whole other world for himself, being part of this other life of rich kids from the private school nearby who treat our restaurant like another McDonald's and not a place you can only afford to go to for a special treat, like most people around here. I bet he imagines driving to Boston to go school shopping instead of having to shop at the crummy outlet mall near our house.

"Fern," he says, expertly kicking another stone across the road. "I need you to promise me something."

"OK," I say. Holden likes me to promise stuff. He's always making me swear to things, like not telling anyone (especially Sara) about the shoe box he keeps full of cutout J.Crew models wearing outfits he tries to copy.

"You have to sit at the front of the bus, behind the driver."

"Isn't that where all the nerds sit?"

He looks up the street again, all tense. "Nah. It's not like that on this bus. Trust me. All the losers sit in the back."

"Really?"

"Yeah, I swear. So when we get on, sit in the second or third row behind the driver. No matter what. Don't pay attention to where I sit, OK? Act like you don't even notice me."

"But – why?"

He won't look at me. "Listen. There's stuff ... stuff you don't understand. People are horrible enough in grade school. But in middle and high school? Those same jerks will look like your best friends compared to the new crop. You have to figure out how to survive.

Sitting at the front of the bus is one way. Pretending you don't know me is another."

"Why not know you?" Holden looks so cool and put together, I can't imagine not wanting to be seen with him.

He sighs. "I just have a feeling. OK?"

I give him the tell-me stare. This is what we call the face-down. It's when we look each other in the eye to see if we're being straight. When our eyes meet, I can see how hard it is for him not to turn away. He looks scared.

"OK," I say. "I promise to sit at the front."

Brakes squeak in the distance, and the top of the bus appears at the end of the road. It looks like a big yellow monster peeking up over a hill. When it stops in front of us, the door folds open. Holden makes me go first. The bus driver looks down at us as we climb the steep steps onto the bus. She has a woolen blue and gold ski hat on, which are our school colours. But instead of our school name, it says TRUDY TRUDY TRUDY all around it. She nods but doesn't say hello. There's sweat beaded at her forehead. I wonder why she's wearing the hat if she's so hot. Maybe she doesn't have any hair underneath. Maybe she has cancer and lost all her hair like Ran's mom. I look away from her and scout out a seat.

The first two seats behind the driver are taken, so I slip into the empty third. I don't turn around to watch Holden, but I can see him in the driver's huge mirror. He's going toward the back, where he said the losers sit.

The second he sits down, two boys in the seat behind him cuff his ears. Holden's face turns bright red.

I can't help it. I swing my head around, desperately wanting to help. But he gives me a death glare that says, *Turn around. Now.* I quickly face forward again, but I can't help watching in the mirror. He stares hard out the window as the two boys lean over the seat and say things in his ears I can't hear. The bus lurches forward, my heart breaking a bit more with each bump in the road. Every time I hear laughter behind me, I cringe.

After a few stops, a girl I've never met before sits next to me. I think she's older. She doesn't say hi, and neither do I. I squeeze the straps on my backpack and try to focus on the dark green vinyl seat in front of me instead of the bus driver's mirror. There's a rip in the seat and someone wrote *F school* below the rip. There's some sort of glue on the rip to try to keep it from tearing anymore, I guess.

F school, I repeat in my head. *F those boys back there.*

When we get to school, I know Holden won't want me waiting, so I follow the crowd inside and start looking for my homeroom.

I feel a hand on my shoulder and swirl around.

"Hey, Fern," Ran says. He smiles the way he always does when we meet up. A certain smile that's just for me.

"Hey," I say.

"You seem sad."

I look down at his chest because I know if our eyes meet, I will cry.

I was wrong about his CHILL T-shirt. Instead, he's wearing a light-green one that says BE in purple letters.

He doesn't take his hand off my shoulder. I wish I could say the words that describe what I'm feeling. But all I can think of is *hurt.*

Our friend Cassie comes over to us and blushes as soon as Ran looks at her. When Ran underwent his transformation from strange sick kid to cool, very cute, and mysteriously-odd-but-in-an-acceptable-way kid, Cassie and every other girl in my class fell in love with him. I think of any of them, Cassie would have had the best chance because:

1. Cassie is really pretty but doesn't act like she knows she is, even if she does.

2. Cassie is nice to everyone, including pre-transformation Ran and me.

3. Like Ran, Cassie is always in a good mood.

Unfortunately for Cassie, she made the mistake of calling him Randy at lunch last year, and ever since he's sort of looked at her in a suspicious way.

"Hey, guys," she says.

"Hey," we both say. She doesn't notice anything is wrong with me. Probably because she is staring at Ran.

"Come on," Ran says. "Let's sit together."

Cassie looks like she might pee her pants in glee. We follow him into our homeroom, where everyone is talking and looking at each other at the same time. Some faces I recognize and some I don't. We sit in the back row, in the corner. I blink to keep from crying and try to take deep breaths. A group of girls in the front stare at Ran, then whisper to each other. Ran is so busy taking notes in his new daily planner, he doesn't even notice.

BE, I think. *Just BE.*

7

AFTER SCHOOL I TAKE MY SAME SEAT on the bus. When Holden gets on, he doesn't even look at me as he heads straight to the back. Sure enough, the same boys sit behind him again. They lean forward and ping his cheek with their fingers. They make kissy faces behind his back. I think about Sara's word. *Fag*. And I wonder how many times he's heard it hissed in his ear.

When the bus stops at our driveway, I get off first and start walking. I don't wait for Holden, knowing I'm supposed to pretend I don't notice him. As soon as the bus pulls away and the sound of the engine drifts off,

I turn to face him. I don't know what I'm going to say, but when I look in his watery eyes, I keep my mouth shut. There's a welt on his left cheek. He walks right by me, past the front walkway, and around the side of the house. I follow, keeping the same distance he put between us on the bus. He disappears into our neighbor's yard and into the pine-tree cave.

When I reach the cave, I stand outside, waiting to be invited in. Waiting and waiting.

"Go home," the cave says.

I bend down to peek inside. His forehead rests on his knees so I can't see his face. But I can tell from the sound of his cracked voice that he's been crying.

"No," I say.

I wait some more.

"Fine," he finally says.

I bend down and crawl in. The familiar smell welcomes me. I sit next to him and look up at the hundreds of crisscross branches above us. They're like interlocking fingers protecting us from the world.

"Well," he says quietly, "how was *your* first day?"

I sigh and think about the rush of my first day of middle school. It was pretty much like any first day of school, except that it was in a new place with twice as many people and every time I had to change classes, at least one person pointed at me and someone else would say The Line in a high-pitched, fake-Charlie voice. When Ran was with me, he acted like he didn't hear anything. I figured I should follow his lead, since no one knows better than Ran how to deal with people giving you a hard time for stuff that is out of your control.

"As expected," I finally say. "You?"

"Pretty much."

"How many people said it to you?" I ask.

"Six, I think. You?"

"At least."

He shakes his head, and we're quiet for a while. But it isn't our usual comfortable quiet. I know the words I need to say aren't the kind we can share without speaking.

"Holden?" I finally say. "Why do you sit at the back of the bus if those jerks do that to you?"

He rubs out the design he was making in the needles with his fingers. "It's complicated."

"I'm not Charlie."

He shakes his head and leans back against the tree trunk, closing his eyes.

"Why do they hurt you?" I ask, leaning next to him.

He's quiet for a long time, then he finally sits up again and puts his back to me. His shirt is covered with needles and pieces of bark.

"I think you know," he says.

I watch the curve of his back rise and fall. I want to touch him and feel his breathing, but I'm afraid I'll feel the hurt. And it seems like a private thing he doesn't want to share. Or maybe he's just protecting me from it.

I think of Sara's words again and Charlie's sing-song echo.

"It's not a good reason," I say.

"No?" He finally turns to me, and I can see the truth in his tears.

"I don't think it is," I say. "People are so stupid."

He smiles a little. "So you don't care? That I'm … you know."

I roll my eyes. "Why would I care? Why should anyone?" But I wonder why neither of us can say the word. *Gay*, I think. *You're gay*. I know what that means. But I don't know how he knows he is, or how it feels, or why people hate him because of it.

"Fern," he says. "You're not like anyone. Other people, they don't get it."

I shrug. "They're idiots."

Holden puts his arms over his bent-up knees and rests his chin on them. "Yeah."

"We have to do something. We could tell Mom and Dad."

"No. Can't you see Mom marching down to the school and causing a scene? And Dad would … I don't know what Dad would do. Try to teach me how to fight or something. Be a man. They'd want to know *why* it happened. And then we'd have to talk about me being…" He pauses and pulls at the rubber on his shoe.

"You can say it," I whisper.

Slowly, he looks up at me. I search his eyes and give him the tell-me stare. He breathes in and out a few times.

"Gay," he says.

I put my hand on his knee. "It doesn't matter," I tell him again. "It doesn't change anything."

He moves his leg away. "It's one thing telling you, but I just don't think I'm ready to officially come out yet, you know? I know Mom will be fine with it. But Dad…"

"They love you. They can help."

"I don't need anyone's *help*," he says, moving even farther away from me.

I lean back against the tree and breathe in Christmas again.

"Yes, you do," I whisper.

My mom always thought I'd be a good friend. A hero, like the *Charlotte's Web* Fern. I would like to be Holden's hero. I really would. I would like to stay his Phoebe forever, so he always has someone to come back to. But when he moves away from me this way, I feel like he's taking a step toward leaving us for good.

8

BACK AT HOME, Sara and my mom are in the kitchen, blasting Grateful Dead tunes and making home-made pasta while Charlie sits on the counter, playing with a ball of dough. There are bits of dough in his hair.

"Ferny!" he yells when he sees me.

"Hi, honey," my mom says, easing a long sheet of dough out of the machine. "Could you set the table?"

"How was school?" Charlie asks, all serious.

My mom folds the pasta and starts to feed it back into the machine. "Oh, right! How was it, Fern? Did you like your classes?"

Sara eyes my outfit. "I take it Holden helped you get ready?"

I look down at my shirt, which I admit is a bit more dressy than what I'd normally wear. Holden forced me to buy it when we went clothes shopping for school.

"What?" I ask her.

"You're twelve, not twenty."

I give her a sneer.

"Snake!" Charlie yells. He holds up a dough snake and makes it wiggle through the air.

"Nice, Charlie!" my mom says, forgetting all about me. "What's his name?"

I grab the stack of dishes and bring them to the table. Instead of going back to the kitchen, I go to my room and spread my homework out on my bed and get to it.

I'm almost done when I hear Charlie's squeaky voice.

"Hi, Ferny," he says, standing in the doorway.

"Hey, Char."

"Wanna play?"

"I'm doing homework."

"I can help."

"I don't think so."

He steps into my room anyway. He's holding Doll, who's wearing one of his old worn-out onesies that is way too big for her. Charlie walks over to the foot of my bed and sets Doll down so she's staring at me.

They wait.

I try to ignore them, but Charlie does this loud breathing thing that drives me crazy. Also, Doll kind of freaks me out with her permanent surprised smile and dirty face.

"Are your hands clean?" I ask.

He holds them up, his fingers spread wide. They're still a little wet.

"OK." I move some of my books out of the way, and he climbs up.

"I wanna go to school," he says.

"School is overrated."

"Huh?"

"Look. All little kids want to go to school. And kindergarten is pretty great. But it just goes downhill from there."

"Oh."

"Enjoy your freedom, bud."

"OK."

He helps me put all my books in a pile, then picks up Doll and follows me downstairs for dinner.

My dad is working late, so it's just my mom and us. He tries to get home for dinner a few nights a week, but lately it happens less and less.

Charlie has separated out all the vegetables from the pasta dish my mom made. He stares at the colourful piles and tells them why he does or doesn't like each one.

"You mushy," he says to an overcooked slice of zucchini.

Holden keeps his head down, close to his plate. He's managed to cover up the welts pretty well. Holden is a master of covering up zits and other imperfections with Sara's old makeup. When Sara was fourteen, she went through this whole makeup stage. She and her friends would have makeup parties and teach each other how to use it. This drove my all-natural mom nuts. She even tried to get them to give each other temporary henna tattoos instead, but none of the other parents would allow it.

One day when Sara wasn't home, Holden and I decided to play dress-up with her stuff. I was about eight and he was ten. We sat on the floor in the bathroom with the carrying case Sara kept all her makeup in spread open between us. I pointed to each colour I wanted to try, then Holden decorated me. I loved the way the powder and lipstick smelled. When I was all done, Holden held out a tiny hand mirror we found in the case. I looked at my Barbie face and laughed. Then I grabbed a blush brush and put some on Holden's cheeks. We were laughing so hard, we didn't hear Sara come up the stairs and down the hall. She stood in the door with her mouth open, hands on hips.

"What are you guys doing!" she screamed. "That's my stuff!" She stomped back down the hall. Holden and I looked at each other and laughed, but we started to put away the makeup.

Before we were done, my mom came upstairs. She looked at me, but she stared at Holden, and I remember how ashamed he seemed. She gave us a lecture about playing with Sara's things without asking and how makeup wasn't a toy. The way she towered above us as we sat on the floor, she looked so big and different. And I felt so small. When she left, we finished putting everything away and looked at each other guiltily. We stood at the sink and quickly washed our faces and then went to our own rooms until it was time for dinner.

Halfway through dinner, my dad asked me what was wrong with my eyes. I rubbed them and some mascara came off on my finger.

"It's my makeup," Sara said.

My dad nodded and smiled at me. "Playing with your sister's stuff?"

I shrugged.

"I think you're much prettier the natural way," he said.

It was the first time he said I was pretty. Maybe it was the first time anyone said I was pretty. I looked across the table at Holden and noticed that his cheeks still seemed red from the blush I'd put there. I touched my cheek and nodded at him carefully to try to let him know. He got the hint right away and got up to go to the bathroom. My dad watched him go.

"I wish you wouldn't let the kids play with that junk," he said to my mom.

"It's not junk," Sara said. "And Mom didn't *let* them. They were sneaking around while I wasn't home."

"Well, whatever," my dad said, still looking at my mom. "I don't like it."

"I don't see why dad cares," I told Holden later. I'd found him hiding out in the pine-tree cave after dinner.

"He thinks I'm weird," Holden said. He wiped his cheeks again as if the makeup were still there.

"Why?" I asked.

"Because I was playing with makeup."

"So what?"

"Boys aren't supposed to."

"That's stupid," I said. "We were just having fun."

But he didn't answer. He just wiped his cheeks again and turned away from me.

Now, sitting at the table watching Holden hide his face, I finally get it. Even then, he knew. And now he's the one who's afraid. Maybe even ashamed. I study my mom as she twirls pasta on her fork. She's pretty open-minded. So is my dad. I'm sure if Holden told them, they'd be supportive. But he stays quiet. So I do, too.

9

THE NEXT MORNING, Holden and I go out to wait for the bus again. Holden teeters at the edge of the road, kicking stones across the street. I join him, imagining that the tiny pebbles are the heads of the jerks who hurt him. Pretty soon we hear the far-off squeal of the bus brakes.

I feel Holden stiffen beside me. "Yeah. You know what? I'm out of here," he says. "Wanna come?"

Yes, I do. But it's only the second day of school.

"Where?" I ask lamely.

"Who cares?"

"What about school?"

"Overrated."

I wonder what Ran would do. He'd probably tell me that running away doesn't mean the problem won't just be waiting when you come back.

The bus brakes sound again. One more stop and we'll see the top of it crest at the hill beyond our house.

I want to go with him. I want to so much.

"You go," I say.

He shrugs and lopes off down the road toward his pine cave, as if he doesn't care a single bit that I don't join him. He doesn't even look back once.

When I step on the bus, I pause at the third seat. It's empty again. Waiting for me. But I keep walking all the way to the back. I keep my jaw clenched as I sit where Holden sat yesterday, in front of the same two boys. The people around me get quiet. It seems like ages before the bus finally starts down the road again.

One of the boys cranes his head close to the back of mine and sniffs.

"Looks like Hildy finally had a sex change," he says.

There's a brief quiet, then everyone around me laughs.

"See you at Hawee's!" someone farther back whines.

I stare straight ahead at first, just like Holden did.

"Hey, Hildy," one of the jerks whispers. "Come back here and sit on my lap."

I feel a hot sting on my ear. One of them has pinged me just like they did to Holden.

My fingers curl into a fist.

"Hey, Hildy, how 'bout a kiss?"

Another ping.

I squeeze my fist tighter. My eyes are watering. How could Holden sit here like this and not *do* something?

"Aw, I think Hildy's gonna cry."

"What's wrong, Hildy? Come back here and I'll make you feel better."

Someone yanks my hair.

"Nope, not a wig!"

I wipe one eye with the back of my hand. *Do not cry. Do not cry.*

"I'm sorry, did that hurt, Hildy?"

Shut up. Shut up, shut up, shut up.

Another tear slips down my face.

"Oh, my God. She's really crying!"

"Maybe she didn't want to be a girl after a—"

The force of my fist against his jaw shuts him up midsentence.

The bus is silent again. I realize there might be a camera in the back of the bus and I'm going to be in serious trouble. Far more than if I'd skipped with Holden. I expect Trudy to pull over and haul me off the bus. But we keep moving on as if nothing happened.

I stay turned around, staring at the jerks. It's funny because I realize they look alike. Thing One and Thing Two. I stare at them and hope they feel my hate burning their skin.

Thing One holds his jaw with a hurt-puppy look on his face.

"You'll regret that," Thing Two says.

I raise my aching fist at him. "You leave my brother alone," I say.

"Oooooh. I'm scared."

"You should be."

He laughs. "You're the one who should be scared. You and your queer brother. I can't believe he needs a little kid to stand up for him. What a wuss."

Thing One doesn't say anything. Maybe my fist managed to do some damage. My fist sure throbs enough. Still, it seems to ache more with the desire to smash Thing Two's nose.

The Things whisper threats in my ear all the way to school. No one sits with me, even though the bus is packed by the time we make the last pickup. I have no idea what the Things are doing behind my back, but I'm sure it's not pretty. I hold my backpack tightly, ready to make a run for it as soon as we get to school. But everyone is up before me, and it's obvious no one is going to let me out of my seat.

I sit back and wait, my cheeks burning. Day two at school and I've officially made enemies with everyone on the bus.

When it's finally my turn to get up, I walk slowly, not knowing what I'll face when I get off. When I reach Trudy, she puts out her hand to stop me. I'm afraid to look her in the eye, so I concentrate on her ugly hat instead. It's grimy and the pom-pom hardly has any yarn left on it.

"You watch yourself, missy," she says. "I know your type. Your brother, too. Troublemakers. I don't stop my bus 'less someone's bleeding normally, but if I see you act up again, you'll be off my bus in a heartbeat."

I feel my mouth drop open in shock.

She makes a face, imitating me.

We stare at each other like that for a few seconds.

Then she moves her pink wrinkled arm, and I nearly fall down the steep steps trying to get away.

Ran's waiting for me at my locker.

"What happened to you?" he asks.

"What do you mean?"

"Well," he says, eyeing me up and down. "You look awful. Why are your ears bright red?"

Ran is wearing a brown shirt that says DIG IT in green letters.

"I don't want to talk about it."

He keeps looking at me anyway. Like Charlie, he knows if he just waits long enough, I'll cave. But I know he'll be disappointed in me if I tell him what I did. Ran is a pacifist. He knows the art of ignoring bullies. I guess Holden does, too.

I hold my sore fist in my other hand.

"I'm fine," I say.

He tilts his head a little to study me.

"OK," he says, as if he knows I'm lying.

He turns to leave. The back of his shirt says COMPOST FOR A CURE, and underneath is a picture of the planet with a Band-Aid on it. As I watch him walk away, I wish he'd come back. I wait for him to turn around, but he just keeps walking.

* * *

At the end of school, I walk slowly to my line for the bus. I swear Trudy gives me the evil eye when I get on. The dirty pom-pom on her hat tips to one side. And the TRUDY TRUDY TRUDY letters feel like a chant. *Trudy's gonna get ya*. I don't know why she hates me. I'm not the one who started it. What about the ear pinging? What about how those jerks treated Holden? She didn't seem to mind *that*.

As I walk past, I look down at the dirty aisle floor. I mean to sit in the third row again, like Holden made me promise, but my legs have other ideas and I'm heading to the back of the bus for more torture. Maybe Holden and I are more alike than I thought.

Things One and Two take their seats behind me. They lean over and grunt in my ears before they sit down.

I look out the window at all the other students waiting in line for the sane buses.

I lean forward and squeeze the straps of my backpack. Exactly fourteen stops before my house. Thirteen. Twelve. The Things don't bother me again, but I swear I can feel their silent insults stinging the back of my head. As we come up over the hill to my house, I slide over to the edge of my seat. But Trudy doesn't slow down. "Hey! You missed the stop!" someone yells.

But the bus keeps chugging down the hill. When we get to the very bottom, she slows and pulls over. I get up and walk down the aisle, careful to watch the floor in case someone sticks out a foot to trip me.

"Sorry 'bout that. Didn't even see you there," Trudy says when I get to the front of the bus.

I start to step down, but she still hasn't opened the door.

"Guess I'm used to looking for your brother," she says in a high-pitched, lispy way just like the Things did when they were talking "gay."

I'm too shocked to reply. The door swings open, and I jump off.

Was this legal? Could she do this? I shake my head as the bus pulls away. Then I look up the long, gradual hill I have to climb. It's September and it's still hot. I stand there, listening to the bus drive away. I wonder if Trudy is checking her mirror to see if I'm walking up the hill yet. Maybe I'll get kidnapped, then rescued somehow. Then my parents could sue Trudy.

As I start to walk, my eyes fill with tears. I feel like a big baby for being so upset, but it really does hurt to be wronged. It hurts so much.

And then I realize. This is probably what Holden feels like every day.

10

No one's home when I finally get to the house. I drop my backpack in the hall by the door and go into the kitchen to pour myself some water. The house feels so quiet, I decide to go back outside and sit on the front steps. The sun blasts down on me, and I feel a drip of sweat slowly slip down my chest and into my belly button under my shirt. I leave my cup on the steps and walk to Holden's tree cave and crawl inside. It's cool and welcoming in a silent way. Holden has wiped the ground smooth, probably so he won't get pine needles on his pants. I sit and listen to the traffic go by. I wish

Holden were here now. Or Ran. But then I think about how disappointed they'd be if I told them what I did on the bus. Holden because I'd broken my promise about sitting in the back, and Ran because I'd used my fists instead of words.

I look at the hand that punched Thing One. I hear the ugly words they hissed in my ears. Feel the sting of their fingers. And I hate them. I hate the way they think.

After a while, my bum starts to get sore from sitting so long, and I climb out of Holden's cave and walk home. Sara, Charlie, and Doll are on the living-room floor, playing Connect Four. My mom is in the kitchen, making dinner.

"Ferny! Come play!" Charlie yells when he sees me. He makes Doll do a happy dance by bouncing her up and down on the rug so it looks like she's jumping.

"No, thanks. I have homework."

"What's up your butt?" Sara asks.

Charlie makes a farting noise.

"Nothing," I say.

She raises her eyebrows. "You're a sucky actress, Fern."

I stop and glare at her. "Do you know about the bus?"

She shifts on the floor. "What do you mean?"

"Do you know what happens on the bus? To Holden?"

"The wheels on the bus go wound and wound," Charlie sings.

"Shut up," I say.

"Bad word!"

I glare at Sara.

"What happens?" she asks. But I have the feeling she has a good idea.

"They hurt him," I say quietly, gesturing toward Charlie to make it clear I can't go into detail in front of him.

She sighs, as if she can't believe she has to explain it all to me. "I didn't ride the bus senior year, but, yeah, I heard that some of the kids gave him a hard time."

"And you didn't do anything?"

"What do you want me to do? I told him to tell Mom and Dad, and he wouldn't."

"So that's it?"

"Yes? Look, what happens on the bus is Holden's problem. Not yours."

"Holden doesn't have a *problem*. They do!"

She flips a red checker into a slot. "He has a problem."

"Stop calling it that!"

79

Charlie claps his hands over his ears.

"Sorry, Fern. But until Holden embraces who he is, it's going to be"—she pauses—"an issue. That's his problem." She drops another checker in a slot. "It's Holden's choice to come out to us and ask for help. He needs to be the one to change things. I only egg him on so he realizes we all know. We all *know*, Fern – me, you, Mom, and Dad. But he's the one who needs to say the words. He has to be the one to take the first step."

"Why?"

"Because that's how it works."

"But what about the bus? Can't you and I do something? Can't we tell Mom—?"

"Tell Mom what?" my mom asks from the doorway.

Sara flashes me a shut-up glare.

"Nothing," I say.

"Holdy has a pwoblem," Charlie says, trying to shove two checkers down a slot.

My mom and Sara exchange a look, and that's when Holden walks in the door.

We all turn toward him. He seems … great. I can't imagine where he's been all day, but he is sort of, well, glowing. He is radiant.

"What's going on?" he asks.

My mom swings her dish towel over her shoulder. "And where have you been all day?"

Holden's face falls. "What do you mean?"

"The school called. You weren't there today."

"Oh."

My mom sighs. "Skipping already, Holden? On the second day? You can't do this, honey."

"What did you tell them? Did you tell them I was home sick?"

My mom shrugs. "I'm not going to do this again, Holden. You've used up your Get Out of Jail Free card today. There are no more."

I can't believe my mom actually covered for him! And from the sound of it, this isn't the first time.

Holden shrugs again. "Thanks."

"We need to talk about why you skipped school on the second day," my mom says.

He looks at me accusingly.

"I didn't say anything!" I say.

My mom turns to me. "You know something about this, Fern?"

The glow on Holden's face is gone.

"Holdy has a pwoblem," Charlie says again, matter-of-factly.

"Shut *up*, Charlie," I say. I turn to Holden. "I swear I didn't."

"Didn't *what*, Fern? What are you two hiding?" my mom asks.

"Just forget it!" Holden storms away and up to his room.

"Come back here!" my mom yells. But his door slams, and we all know he's not coming back. She comes closer to me. "Are you going to fill me in on what's going on?"

I shake my head, even though I want to tell her. I want to make her fix it. But I promised.

"Sara?" she asks.

"You need to ask him," she says. But instead of going upstairs, my mom goes back to the kitchen.

"Ferny, you play with me," Charlie says from the floor.

Sara bolts up before I can answer. "Have fun!" she says, sauntering into the kitchen after my mom.

Charlie pushes the trap that releases the checkers, laughing as they clank on top of each other into a heap. But I hardly pay attention. Am I the only one who cares that Holden is upset?

"Me first!" Charlie whines.

I guess so.

11

AT DINNER, Holden doesn't look at me. At any of us. He probably wouldn't have even come to dinner, but my dad's home, and, unlike my mom, my dad would never let Holden get away with skipping a family meal.

I watch my dad take a bite of my mom's sesame tofu and green-bean salad. He makes the strangest face as he chews, as if he's trying to guess what he's eating. I notice my mom watching him closely, almost challenging him to complain. Sometimes I think the reason he stays at the restaurant during dinner isn't because it's so busy but because it means he can have a tofu-free meal.

"So, how's school going so far, you two?" he asks. He moves two tofu chunks to the side of the plate. It reminds me of something Charlie would do.

"Same ol' same ol'," Holden says quietly.

I look over at my mom to see if she'll rat Holden out, but she pretends to concentrate on cutting Charlie's food.

"What about you, Ferny?" my dad asks.

I shrug.

"Jeez. Why is everyone so gloomy?"

Charlie drops his spoon and smiles an amazingly sweet smile at my dad. His mouth opens wide, and a piece of tofu falls out.

"That's disgusting," I say.

Charlie frowns. His bottom lip starts to quiver the way it always does before he cries.

"Fern, honestly," my mom says. "Do you have to be so mean to him?"

What?

I look over to Holden for help and remember he's mad at me, too. I bite my own lip to keep it from quivering.

"OK, something's going on here, and I want to know what," my dad says.

We're all quiet.

"I'm waiting."

Finally Holden puts his fork down. "Apparently everyone thinks I have a problem."

"Honey, of course we don't," my mom says in her usual calm way.

"It was just a misunderstanding," Sara adds.

"It was!" I say.

Holden pushes back his chair.

"Where do you think you're going?" my dad asks.

"Away from here." He stands up.

"Holden," I say. "It's not what you think. We were just talking about—"

"Me. Behind my back."

"No! Well, yes, but—"

He doesn't wait to hear more. He stomps to the front door and slams it shut behind him.

"Does someone want to tell me what that was all about?" my dad asks.

No one does.

He looks at each of us, but we all pretend to get very interested in our food.

"We'll talk later," my mom says quietly.

* * *

After dinner, I call Ran. I want to tell him everything that happened, but for some reason I just don't have the energy. Instead, we talk about our new math teacher, Mr. Hand. Ran says that Mr. Hand seems very smart and that we're going to learn a lot this year. He tells me that geometry is very abstract. I don't even know what that means, but it feels good to just listen to Ran's calm voice. Ran never gets worried about anything. He has this thing he calls a mantra. "All will be well," he's always saying. I think a lot of other people would think this made Ran kind of a freak. But when he tells me all will be well, it calms me and makes me believe it. And now I realize how badly I need to hear those words.

"I had a really awful day today," I tell him when he finally stops listing the benefits of geometry.

"Tell me."

So I explain about the bus and Holden and the Things, and getting dropped off too far from the stop. When I finish, he's quiet for a little while. I listen to him breathing, thinking.

"Fern," he finally says, "you've had a hard day. But all will be well."

I take a deep breath in and out, too. As if I am trying to breathe in his words.

"I really don't want to ride the bus tomorrow," I tell him.

"Then don't."

"But how will I get to school?"

"Where there's a will, there's a way," he tells me, as if it's that simple.

"Which is?"

"I'm not sure. But you'll figure it out." I can tell he's ready to end our conversation, because he always changes his tone of voice. It gets slower and quieter. As if he's reading me a bedtime story.

"All will be well," he says again. "Remember."

"OK," I say. I want to make him promise. "Thanks."

"You're welcome," he answers quietly. "Good night." I try to stay up until I hear Holden come back in, but the next thing I know, Charlie is rapping on my door, telling me it's time to get ready for school. I hear him run down the hall and do the same on everyone else's door. If I did that, Sara and Holden would kill me.

Downstairs I start to eat a fake Pop-Tart. When my mom bought them, she insisted they would taste just like the "bad" kind. I start to chew and gag on the cardboard-tasting organic crust. I quickly grab Charlie's juice cup and swallow it down.

"Noooooo, Fern!!" Charlie wails. "Mooommmmyyyy!"

By now I am in no mood to make things right, so I dump the cup in the sink and get him a new one just as my mom drags herself into the kitchen.

"What now?" she asks.

"Fern stole my juice!" Charlie cries.

"I was *choking*!" I say. "Don't be such a baby."

"Oh, honestly, Fern. He *is* a baby."

"He's *three*!"

Charlie sniffs. "You not nice, Ferny."

"Don't call me Ferny," I say. "I'm sick of it."

"Fern," my mom says, disgusted.

Charlie bangs his new cup on his high chair, which he is way too big for.

"Where's Holden?" my mom asks.

"In the shower." I go to the downstairs bathroom to brush my teeth. In our house, you have to have stuff like toothbrushes in both bathrooms in case one is occupied and you're in a hurry. When I'm done, I leave the house without saying good-bye.

I wait alone at the end of the driveway. I try to kick a stone across the road but stub my toe on the pavement instead. I'm probably the only person in history to stub her toe on a flat surface.

The screen door slams up at the house. Holden walks toward me with his head tucked down, his hands in his pockets. When he reaches the end of the driveway, he kicks a pebble across.

"Don't be mad at me," I say.

He's quiet.

"We weren't talking about you in the way you think."

"What way were you talking about me, then?"

"We were just…" I can't figure out how to explain. He's right. We were talking about him behind his back. And probably no way is a good way.

"Never mind," I say. "I'm sorry."

He sighs and goes to the side of the driveway to find more pebbles to kick. He sends one sailing across the pavement and into the grass on the other side. A dog in our neighbor's yard barks and comes over, but he can't get too close because of the invisible fence they put up. He eyes the spot where the stone landed and whimpers.

"Poor ol' trapped thing," Holden says.

He looks both ways and crosses the street, then finds a stick near a tree and throws it to the dog, who catches it perfectly. He drops it just at the edge of where the fence must be and wags his tail. "Sorry, bud. That's all I have time for," he says, and walks back over to me.

"So, how was the ride without me yesterday?" he asks.

"What do you think?"

"Same ol' same ol'?"

"Not exactly."

"No?"

"I punched Thing One in the face."

His mouth drops open. "Thing One?"

"Yeah. That's what I call those jerks who hassle you. I took your seat yesterday, and they said stuff to me I didn't like. So, I punched one of them."

"Are you *crazy*?"

I shrug.

"What'd they do after?"

"Nothing. Just gave me dirty looks."

He shakes his head. "What about Trudy? She didn't kick you off for belting one of her nephews?"

This time *my* mouth drops open. "Her nephews?"

"Yeah. Austin and Tyler McCready. She's their aunt."

The familiar squeal of brakes sounds in the distance.

"We can't get on that bus," I say. "No wonder she skipped our stop yesterday."

"What do you mean?"

"She drove past our stop. She waited till she got all the way down the hill before she pulled over so I had to walk up."

"She's evil. You're lucky she didn't kick you off the bus forever."

"That would have been great! Then we wouldn't have to ride it anymore. Anyway, I bet she can't because the video on the bus would show her nephews pinging my ears before I belted one of them."

"They did *what*?"

"You know." I ping the air to show him.

He looks up and down the road. "We gotta get out of here."

"You can't skip again. Mom and Dad will kill you."

"Who said anything about skipping? We just need to find a different way to get to school. Come on."

He runs back up the driveway, kind of hunched over, as if that will actually prevent anyone from seeing him. I follow.

By the side of the garage, we pant, catching our breath while the bus drives by.

"Why don't we just ask Dad for a ride? He hasn't left for work yet, right? Or Mom?"

"No," Holden says. "Too much explaining."

"Sara?"

He cringes. Sara has her license, just no car. She could easily drive us and be back in time for her, my mom, and Charlie to get to the restaurant.

"She's our only hope," I say.

"OK. But just tell her we missed the bus, all right?"

"She's annoying, not stupid."

He rolls his eyes. "Whatever. Just don't bring it up. She's so smug. I don't want her to feel like she's saving us."

"Fine." I peek through the kitchen window. My mom is putting jam on an English muffin, and Charlie is drinking from his new cup. I duck down and race to the back door, where I can slip in and go up to Sara's room.

She's sound asleep. Her room smells like five different kinds of incense and too much patchouli. I gag. She rolls over and opens her eyes.

"Wha?"

"We need your help," I say.

"Who?" she asks groggily.

"Me and Holden."

She sits up and scratches her head. She scratches her head a lot. I think it's because of the dreadlocks. Honestly, if you look at them too closely, they are kind of disgusting.

"What is it?" she asks.

"We need a ride to school."

"Take the bus."

"We can't. We, uh … missed it."

She eyes me suspiciously.

"We can't take it anymore," I say. "I did something."

"*You?*"

That hurt.

"What did you do?"

"I don't have time to explain. Can you just please give us a ride? And don't tell Mom?"

She sighs. "All right, fine. I'll be there in five minutes. But don't expect me to do this every day."

I don't tell her that's exactly what I expect. But we can deal with that later. I sneak back out of the house and find Holden leaning against the side of the garage, staring at his shoes.

"She's coming," I say.

He nods. "I knew she'd come through."

For a second I feel this strange jealous twinge. *But I'll always be your favourite, right?* I want to say. But I don't, because Sara arrives and we all get into the car.

"You're wearing too much cologne," Sara says to Holden after we've safely pulled out of the driveway.

I sit forward from the backseat and sniff. She has a point. I roll down my window a crack.

Holden adjusts the front seat so he can lean back, all casual.

"You think I'm going to do this every day now, don't you?" Sara says.

"Yes," he answers.

"Are you going to tell me what really happened?"

I think this is the longest they've gone without arguing or being mean to each other. It feels weird.

"Fern punched one of Trudy's idiot nephews in the face yesterday."

The car swerves as Sara looks at me in the rearview mirror in shock. "Fern! Are you crazy? I didn't know you were violent!"

Holden turns around and points at me. "Fern's violent," he says, and cracks up.

"Shut up. I only did it because of you."

"That was very wrong," Sara says, imitating our dad. "God, I wish I could have seen that. Did you get him good? Which one was it?"

I look at the slight bruises on the knuckles of my right hand and feel a twinge of pride. "I got him pretty good. I don't know which one it was. They look the same."

Sara shakes her head. "Heh. Yeah, well, twins are like that. Wow, Tooty must have totally freaked out."

"Tooty?"

"Yeah, that's what we used to call her 'cause the bus reeked so bad. Does she still wear her stupid hat?"

"Uh-huh."

"Wow, Ferny. Punching Tooty's nephew in the face. I never knew you had it in you."

I lean back in the seat again and look out the window. I feel my mouth turn into a smile. *Me, either,* I think.

12

RAN IS WAITING FOR ME at my locker. Today his T-shirt says BEHOLD.

"Did you take the bus?" he asks.

"Nope," I say.

He smiles. "I knew you'd figure it out!"

Cassie comes dashing over to join us.

"Behold," Cassie says, staring at his chest.

"Yes," Ran says.

Cassie glances at me. I shrug. What Cassie doesn't understand is that Ran isn't the kind of person you ask, "Why?" He wants you to figure things out for yourself.

I stuff my bag in my locker and grab my books. "Come on. We're going to be late."

I spend the day at school rushing from class to class, hoping I won't pass the Things in the halls and kicking myself for not realizing I'm still going to have to take the bus *home*. During last period, I have study hall. The class is packed. Our teacher's name is Mrs. Drabble, but everyone calls her Mrs. Dribble because she's old and has a reputation of falling asleep at her desk and drooling. Ran has vowed that if this happens, he will wake her up. Cassie thinks that is very heroic of him. Of course.

Today Mrs. Dribble has a thermos on her desk that she sips from almost exactly every two minutes. Mrs. Dribble is also known for screaming at you if you talk during study hall, so everyone is very quiet. You can practically hear the electric clock slowly buzzing the second hand forward. I count down the minutes until I will be sitting on the bus with the Things. Twenty-seven. I look over at Ran, who is writing something fast and furious in his tiny journal. He calls it his idea book. He must have a pretty good one.

Cassie sits behind him reading her social studies book and taking notes. Every so often she leans forward as if she's trying to look over Ran's shoulder and read from his journal. I'm sure Ran notices, which is another reason Cassie is doomed when it comes to her chances with him.

I try to concentrate on my geometry homework for a while, but the numbers blur together. I switch to English, but I keep reading the same paragraph over and over again. I stare at the clock. I swear the minute hand is moving backward. I watch Mrs. Dribble take a sip from her thermos and wonder what's in there that makes her smile just a tiny bit after every sip.

Twelve minutes.

When the bell finally rings, I nearly get trampled as everyone makes a run for the door. The halls are so crowded, I can barely make my way to my locker.

"Are you taking the bus?" Ran asks as we move along in the sea of students toward the pickup area.

I nod.

"Be strong," he says, and lets himself get pushed along to his own bus line. "All will be well!" he yells to me as he's carried away.

I look around for Holden, but I don't see him anywhere. The Things are at the front of the line, pushing each other.

Someone grabs my arm and pulls me out of the line.

"Come on, let's get out of here."

Holden pulls me backward until we're free from the crowd. A guy in a black Volkswagen Bug rolls down his window when we get to the parking lot.

"Hey," he says.

"This is my little sister. Can we drop her off at my parents' restaurant?"

"No problem," the guy says.

Holden opens the door and tilts the seat up for me. The car smells like Sara's bedroom. Like incense but like cigarettes, too. As we pull out of the parking lot, the guy turns around. He looks a lot older than Holden.

"I'm Gray," he says.

"Fern."

"Cool name. Like the plant?"

"Like the girl. In *Charlotte's Web*." My cheeks burn.

"The movie?"

"The book."

"Dude," he says to Holden. "Your parents are whacked. Did they name all of you after book characters?"

"They're kind of eccentric," Holden says quietly.

"That's so cool. Too bad you got named after that depressed kid, though."

"Yeah," Holden says. "Tell me about it."

"You got a good one, though," he says to me. "A pig saver!"

Terrific.

I try to smile, but some things you can't force.

"Although…" Gray says, "if I remember correctly, it's really that spider who saves the pig. In the end, I mean."

"Fern saves him first," Holden says.

"Riiiight." Gray turns up the volume and nods his head to the music. Holden copies him. I look out the window.

Fern. What kind of a lame name is that? What were my parents thinking, naming me after a kid whose only friend was a pig marked for death?

At the restaurant, Gray pulls up near the front door, and Holden leans forward with the seat to let me out. "See you later," he says. He has the glow again.

"Thanks for the ride," I tell Gray.

"No prob." He's still tapping his fingers on the steering wheel, even though he turned off the music.

After they drive off, I stand in front of the

restaurant and look up at the huge Harry's sign towering over me. I never actually met the real Harry, my grandfather. My grandparents died just two months apart. My grandmother died first from cancer and then my grandfather from a heart attack. My mom says it was really a broken heart. We used to have a bunch of photos of them hanging in the restaurant, but that caused confusion once my dad started letting on that *he* was Harry. People wanted to know who the old couple was, and that meant my dad would have to admit he was a big fake. Sometimes I wonder if my mom sees my dad as a phony the way the Holden in her favourite book sees other people. I hope not.

I notice my reflection in the huge window in front of the restaurant. I look like a stranger standing here. I look small.

A tiny head pops up at the bottom of the window from inside. It has bushy brown hair. A little hand spreads across the glass and waves slowly.

I smile and wave back.

Inside, the restaurant's familiar sweet and greasy smell wraps around me. Charlie is sitting at the table under the window with Doll. Doll's hair has been twisted into dreadlocks and dyed green. Charlie must have fallen asleep with his face against her because the side of his cheek is green, too.

"Where's Mom?" I ask, looking around at the empty dining room. The restaurant is still pretty dead during the lull between lunch and the rush of the early-bird special at dinner. I sit across from Charlie at the Formica table. My dad bought the tables from different diners that were going out of business. He thinks people like to be reminded of old-fashioned diners. He says things that make people nostalgic make them happy. The booth seats are red vinyl, and you have to be careful if you sit on them wearing shorts or you'll leave a layer of skin when you get up. At least it feels that way.

Charlie wraps Doll in his blanket and sets her on the table. Then he holds his hands out and pinches his fingers as he closes his eyes and says, "Ommmm." This is his way of telling me that my mom is upstairs meditating.

"Where's Sara?"

He shrugs.

I look around again at the empty room. "Who's supposed to be watching you?"

"Mona. But I a big boy."

"Well, where is she?"

"Potty."

The tiny bell on the door jingles, and an enormous woman and man walk in with a skinny kid. Since no one else is around, I go over and say hello and ask if they're here for lunch or ice cream.

The couple looks at me closely. Then the lady gets this big grin on her face. "I recognize you!" she says. She looks around the room and spots Charlie kissing Doll. "And there's that adorable little girl! The one who says 'See you at Hawee's!'"

Oh, brother.

"Look, Justina," she says to the skinny kid. "Remember the commercial?" She turns to me. "We saw your commercial on the TV in our camper and thought it'd be a hoot to come here. We're kind of ice-cream connoisseurs. We travel all over and try different kinds. We just went on the tour at Ben & Jerry's in Vermont last week. Is your ice cream better than theirs?"

I stare at her. What is it with tourists watching TV in their RVs? Aren't they supposed to be looking out the windows and enjoying nature or something?

"Um…"

"Does it matter where we sit?" she asks, sort of waddling around me.

I grab three menus and follow them. They take the booth next to Charlie, but before they sit down, the woman reaches into her gigantic purse and pulls out a cell phone. "You don't mind if I take your picture, do you? Oh! Maybe your little sister could say her line for me. My phone has video."

Charlie hugs Doll to his chest and eyes the lady suspiciously, which he often does when strangers say he's cute.

The lady turns to him. "Do you know your line? From the commercial?"

Charlie looks at me.

"See you at Harry's," I mumble at him.

"I don't talk to stwanjahs," he tells the lady in a baby voice. Then he dashes across the dining room and hides behind the ice-cream counter.

"Oh, my, I scared her," the lady says, as if Charlie is some wild animal.

"It's OK," I say. I hand out the menus and hope she forgot about the photo. "Someone will be with you to take your order in just a minute."

I head to the counter and grab Charlie's hand.

Together we go up to my dad's office to find my mom. The door is closed, with my mom's go-away sign flipped over. Nice.

Charlie presses his ear against the door. "I hear the singing bowl!" he whispers loudly.

I roll my eyes. "C'mon, then. Let's find Sara."

We go back downstairs and wander through the kitchen, but she's not there, either. Patrick, the head cook, says she was just here but went somewhere with Gil, the busboy. "Try the walk-in," he tells us.

Charlie stiffens beside me. He hates the walk-in. It's cold and smells like rotting vegetables most of the time, so I don't really blame him. "C'mon, I'll protect you," I say.

Just as I'm about to open the door, Sara pushes it open from the other side.

"Oh!" she says. "What are you doing here?"

Charlie reaches for her hand. "You cold," he says, letting go.

"Well, yeah. It's a refrigerator."

Gil comes out behind her carrying a plastic bin full of sliced onions. Charlie points at his head and laughs.

"What?" he asks.

His hair is sticking straight up. Sara pats it down for him.

"We were just helping Patrick with dinner prep," Sara says.

I look at her suspiciously. Since when does Sara ever help? "You're supposed to be watching Charlie," I say.

Sara picks him up, but he squirms to get down and hugs my legs. "Mona said she'd watch him for a bit."

"Well she *wasn't*," I say.

"Oh, Fern, calm down. Everyone looks out for Charlie."

"There are customers in the dining room waiting to order. They wanted to take our *picture*."

She sighs. "All right, I'll handle it."

"Need help?" Gil asks her.

"No," she says coldly. She leaves us standing there as she marches out to the dining room. Charlie runs after her.

As soon as Gil takes the cover off the onions, the smell is overpowering. I decide to escape through the back door before Sara can get me to take the ice-cream order. When I open the door, I nearly plow into my dad, who's standing there talking to a tiny man wearing a Red Sox cap. He's eating an ice-cream cone.

"Oh, hey, here's my daughter Fern. One of the stars of the show," my dad says, hugging me close to him.

The guy nods at me and licks his cone.

"So we could start with just the local stores," my dad continues as if I'm not there. "And then we'll move from there. We've got to start small. Make it hard to get. A specialty item. And maybe we could use a spot from the commercial on the label, you know? So people recognize it. Like I did with the truck. Did you see the truck out front?"

The guy looks bored. "Uh-huh." He licks his cone again.

"It'll be just like Ben and What's-His-Name," my dad continues. "And I'm thinking we should use an image from the ad, like I said. Only with the whole family, not just Charlie."

I look up at him.

Say what?

"You know, with all of us standing under the sign. Wouldn't that be great?"

He squeezes me tighter, clearly thinking I'm going to share his excitement about this latest brilliant idea. Sure, Dad. Our family photo on pints of ice cream at every store in town? Oh, yeah. That would be faaaaantastic.

13

AT DINNER THAT NIGHT, I pick at my garlic mashed potatoes while Sara tries to explain why my dad must not, under any circumstance, put our picture on an ice-cream label. I make a butter pond in my potatoes and slowly sacrifice overcooked lima beans into the butter water. Every time Sara raises her voice, Charlie bangs his feet against his high chair and chants, "See you at Hawee's!"

My dad seems to think this is hysterical. "I can always count on you, bud, can't I?" he says, looking around at the rest of us disappointedly. He reaches across the table to ruffle Charlie's hair. He pulls his hand away and makes a face, then wipes mashed potato off his fingers. Sara catches my eye, and we share smirks.

"Where's Holden, anyway?" my dad asks.

My mom looks at the clock, then at me. I shrug. I don't think Holden was expecting my dad to be home for dinner two nights in a row.

"As I was saying," Sara goes on, "I don't understand why you can't just use Charlie's photo, Dad. Like the one on the truck."

"This is a *family* restaurant, Sara. *Family.* I want us all to take part. We're a team!"

"I thought team members got a say in their strategy," she says.

"Think of me as the team captain. The team captain knows what's best."

Oh, brother. I continue to drown all of my lima beans and wait for Sara to give a good comeback, but then Holden walks through the front door.

"Sorry I'm late!" he says cheerfully, and disappears into the kitchen. He returns with a huge pile of mashed potatoes on his plate.

"Why are *you* in such a good mood?" Sara asks.

"None of your business," he says, cramming his mouth full of potato. "Mmm, Mom. These are fantastic."

"Well, you won't be so happy when you find out what Dad's been up to," Sara says.

Holden stops chewing.

"Oh, Sara, don't be so dramatic," my mom says.

"Dad's putting our picture on ice-cream cartons that are going to be for sale in all the grocery and convenience stores," I tell Holden. "Our picture from the *commercial*."

Holden practically chokes on his potatoes. "*Why?*"

"That's what I said!' Sara agrees. "I'm eighteen. That means I have to give my permission for anyone to use my image. Right, Mom? I mean, legally? Fern, Holden, and Charlie are minors, so you have to make the decision whether or not you want to exploit them, but you can't exploit me!"

"What's essploit?" Charlie asks.

"Daddy's not exploiting anyone," my mom says.

"That's exactly what he's doing! Doesn't he realize how *bad* we all look? I mean, give me a break! At least if he wants to use us, let us retake the photo so we look halfway decent."

"Am I not sitting at this table?" my dad asks.

"Why can't you just use the picture of Charlie that's on the truck?" Holden asks him.

"See?" Sara asks. "Charlie's the perfect solution."

Charlie blows a raspberry at her. I'm sure he would've wiggled his bum, too, if he wasn't trapped in his high chair.

"Fern," my dad says, "you've been pretty quiet about all of this. How do you feel?"

Everyone looks at me, as if they just now realize I am sitting at the table, even though I spoke six seconds ago.

My mom eyes my butter pond with disgust.

"I like the Charlie idea," I say. "No offense, but we looked pretty lame in that ad. Sorry, Dad."

He shakes his head. "What is happening to this family? What happened to our team?"

"Go, team!" Charlie yells.

"Maybe we should vote," my mom suggests.

My dad's face is getting redder by the minute. I feel bad for disappointing him, but when I picture our hideous family photo in the freezer of every convenience and grocery store in town, I can't bring myself to take his side.

"Never mind." My dad gets up and clears his plate. My mom follows.

"Down!" Charlie says.

Sara pushes his high chair back, and he slides out and runs toward the kitchen after my parents.

"You could have been a little nicer," I say.

"It was the only way to make him listen, Fern. Dad just goes too far. All he cares about is the business."

"Even so," I say. I pick up my plate and head to the kitchen, too.

The thing is, my dad is the kind of person who gets carried away. When he thinks he has a good idea, there's just no stopping him. We all know he doesn't only care about the business. But sometimes ... yeah. Sometimes it does sort of feel that way.

14

THE NEXT DAY, Sara gets up and drives us to school without being asked. Ran is waiting for me at my locker as usual. Cassie sees us from a few lockers down and comes rushing over. "Hey, guys," she says. "Great shirt."

Ran's shirt is hot pink and says GO WITH THE FLOW.

"Thank you," he says.

For some reason, none of us has anything else to say, so we start to walk toward homeroom. We're almost there when I see the Things headed our way.

"Uh-oh," I say. I move closer to Ran.

"Hey, Hildy," one of them says. "Is this your boyfriend?"

Ran stops in the middle of the hall to face them. People bump into us, but gradually the traffic swerves around us. Cassie looks like she wants to crawl into a locker. I would like to join her.

"Nice shirt," Thing One says to Ran in his stupid "gay" voice.

"Thanks," Ran says. He is so calm and cool.

"Excuse us." I take Ran's arm and start to lead him away.

Shockingly, the Things step aside, and the three of us walk on.

"See you at Hawee's!" they call after us. But this time, I don't cringe. Ran, Cassie, and I look at each other and crack up. Somehow, with Ran around, stuff like that just seems so stupid.

"What losers," Cassie says, laughing.

Ran gets a weird look on his face but doesn't say anything. I'm sure he would like to, but he has a thing about negativity. He's always trying to figure out *why* people act like jerks instead of just letting them be jerks. I'm sure it's something his parents used to have him do when he was still getting bullied. "Sometimes if you make up a really sad story for them, it's easier not to take them being mean to you so personally," he told me once.

When Cassie realizes Ran isn't going to agree with her, she blushes. I feel sorry for her because I know she's going to kick herself again for saying the wrong thing. I wish she would just take the hint that maybe if she is always saying things Ran doesn't like, they wouldn't make the best couple in the world. Besides, why can't we just all stay friends? Them being a couple would ruin everything. And I don't think that because I think maybe Ran and I could be ... well, never mind. It just would.

"They seem pretty secure to me," I say, hoping to make Cassie feel a little better.

"Looks can be deceiving," Ran says.

Well, he would know.

After school, Holden waves to me, and I follow him to the curb, where we wait for Gray. Ran walks over to us and asks if he can come, too. Holden shrugs. When Gray pulls up, we climb in.

"Who's the new guy?" Gray asks.

"This is my friend Ran," I tell him.

"Cool." He turns up the music, and Ran and I lean back in our seats. Once we're on the road, Gray reaches over and takes Holden's hand as if it is the most natural thing in the world. They start singing to the song on the radio at the top of their lungs. It's like they're friends and boyfriends at the same time. It's the first time I've seen Holden look so happy. So comfortable. It's like he's a whole new person. I wish he could always be like this. Who he really is.

When Gray drops us off, Ran and I stand in front of the restaurant. "Gray seems nice," Ran says. "They make a good couple." That's Ran. I knew it wouldn't faze him a bit to see Holden hold hands with a guy. "But he does seem kind of old, doesn't he? How old do you think he is?"

"I don't know," I say. I'm surprised Ran even cares. He never cares about stuff like that.

The door opens and Charlie comes tearing out at top speed. He flies right into Ran's open arms. Ran lifts him in the air and almost falls over.

"I love you, Wan!" Charlie giggles.

"Nice to see you, too," I say.

Charlie gives me a bashful look. "Hi, Ferny."

He takes Ran's hand and leads us inside. There are a few customers, but mostly the restaurant is pretty dead. Ran and I try to do our homework, but Charlie keeps interrupting us.

"Where're Mom and Sara?" I ask, noticing for the first time that Mona is the only one taking orders.

Charlie makes a meditation pose.

"Again?" I ask.

He nods.

"What about Sara?"

"Helping Gil." He crawls into Ran's lap and starts to inspect his ear.

"Since when does Sara help Gil?"

Charlie just shrugs.

When my mom finally comes down, she heads straight to a table in the back with the big silverware bin and starts wrapping sets of forks, knives, and spoons in napkins for dinner prep. Charlie runs over to help. She giggles with him, and they chatter away as they stack the bundles into a fort around Doll, who sits on the table with her green dreadlocks and shocked expression. When I was Charlie's age, my mom never talked to me like that. I spent most of my time making my own forts under the tables with Holden. I guess the two of us have always needed our hideouts. Even when we were little.

After what feels like hours, it's finally time to go home. My mom scoops Charlie up and squeezes him tight. "Ran, do you have any dinner plans?" she asks.

Ran smiles. "Actually, my dad's working late."

"Come on home with us, then," she says.

At dinner my mom tells us that my dad is at some special meeting, and she does *not* want to talk about it. I'm sure it's about the stupid ice-cream labels.

Dinner is vegetarian shepherd's pie. The fake meat is chewy and weird, and the only one who seems to like it is Ran.

"So, tell us about Gray," Sara says to Holden. "What's he like, anyway?"

"None of your business," Holden says.

"Who's Gray?" my mom asks.

Sara smiles. "Holden's new friend."

"Oh?"

Holden flashes my sister a warning look. "Yeah," he tells my mom.

"He's nice," I say.

"Fern and I were wondering how old he is," Ran says. I kick him under the table, and he looks at me like he genuinely doesn't know why. "I was just wondering," he adds quietly. "Because he seemed kind of old."

"Old?" my mom asks.

"He's in high school like me," Holden says. "Jeez, Ran."

"What?"

"Never mind."

"What grade?" my mom asks.

"Senior," Holden mumbles toward his plate.

"A *senior*?"

"Wow!" Sara says. "An older man."

I picture Gray and Holden holding hands. "He's really nice," I say again. "He doesn't seem that old to me."

"Is he from Union? Maybe I know him," Sara says. "I mean, since I'm only a year older than him."

"You don't know him. He's from the Academy," Holden says.

"The Academy? Really? How did you meet?" my mom asks.

Ran's head flips back and forth between each family member as if he's watching a tennis match.

"What is this, the third degree?" Holden asks. "It's none of your business!"

"I'm only your mother."

"And this is my life, not yours! We're not a show!" Holden picks up his plate and storms out of the dining room.

My mom sighs in her usual way. Like she's disappointed and frustrated but it's best to let him go. She's always just letting him run off. Just once I would like to see her go after him and hug him like she hugs Charlie every five minutes. Just once I would like her to hug *me*.

"He's so sensitive," Sara says.

"Are they boyfriends?" my mom whispers.

"Why don't you ask him?" I say. I remember what Sara told me, about how Holden needs to be the one to tell us he's gay. But maybe he could use some help. Maybe if my mom would just try to talk with him, he'd open up. But instead of responding, she starts to clear the table.

Ran thanks her for dinner, and I walk him outside while we wait for his mom to come pick him up.

"That was an interesting dinner," he says.

"I can think of a better word for it."

"Like what?"

"Sucky?"

"That's not a word."

I elbow him. "I just wish my mom weren't *so* laid-back, you know? I wish she'd talk to him."

"Maybe she's afraid of what he'll say."

"Well, yeah. But the thing is, I don't get what she's so afraid of."

His mom pulls into the driveway. "Don't worry," he tells me before he gets into the car. "All will be well."

I wish I could believe it.

Later, as I head toward my room to escape having to play Connect Four with Charlie, I pass by Holden's bedroom door and hear him talking to someone.

"I could come see you now," he says. "Yeah. I'll just sneak out. No problem. My family is totally clueless."

Slowly, I inch closer to his doorway. He's lying on his back, knees bent, on top of his perfectly made bed. "You could come pick me up. I could meet you at the end of the street.... I know. I'll get my license next year."

That is a total lie, since Holden is only fourteen.

I hear Sara coming up the stairs and hurry to my room. I shut the door and lie on my bed, staring at my slanted ceiling where I picked the wallpaper when I was little. Holden's voice sounded so pleading. So different from today in the car. He sounded like he wanted to escape from us so badly.

My family is totally clueless.

Not all of us are, I think. *We love you. You're the one who's too clueless to notice.*

15

OUR SCHOOL ROUTINE IS NOW THIS: Sara brings us to school, and Gray picks us up. Sometimes Ran comes to the restaurant with me and sometimes he doesn't. One thing I notice about the restaurant is that it seems to be getting even busier. During the once-dull time between lunch and dinner, my dad comes out from the back to chat with new customers and fill them in on his version of Harry's "history." Sometimes when it gets really busy, he asks me to help scoop ice cream. Even though Sara is supposedly working out back, helping Gil and Patrick, it's not clear what she's actually doing.

Mostly she just comes out to the dining room, steers people looking for ice cream over to the counter, and then disappears before they can order a cone. As for my mom, she seems to spend more and more time trying to find her inner peace in the upstairs office. I think the busier the restaurant gets, the deeper her peace goes into hiding.

On one particularly busy day, I'm helping scoop when someone says, "Hey! That's the girl from the commercial!"

I groan. Here we go again.

At that moment, Charlie comes racing around the counter and hugs my leg, making me almost drop the cone I'm holding.

"And there's the little girl who says 'See you at Harry's!'" someone yells.

"No, it's 'See you at *Hawee's*!'" someone else says.

Everyone laughs.

Charlie squeezes my leg tighter.

I hobble to the counter with Charlie attached to my leg and hand the cone to some old guy. I feel the eyes in the line looking at me.

A tiny kid pops his head up to the counter and peeks at me. "Can I have your autograph, please?" he asks.

You've got to be kidding me. I look at Trevor the dishwasher/ice-cream scooper. He shrugs.

"Um, I guess so," I say.

The boy slides over a napkin. I grab a pen off the counter and start to sign my name. But writing on a napkin with a ballpoint pen doesn't really work, so I end up tearing the paper a little. It looks horrible, but I slide it back to the kid anyway.

He frowns. "Thanks a lot," he says in this ungrateful way.

"Where's Sara?" I ask Charlie.

"Helping Gil," he says.

"And Mom?"

He points upstairs.

Typical. For someone who is invisible, why am I the only one in this family who can't seem to master the art of disappearing?

When I finish helping Trevor with the rush, Charlie and I go in search of Sara and my mom. We're just heading up the stairs to my dad's office as my mom, Sara, and Gil come out of the room. Sara's and Gil's cheeks are bright red.

"What's wrong?" Charlie asks.

My mom glances at Sara and Gil. "Nothing, baby.

I was just having a chat about work with Sara and Gil."

You mean like how they don't do any? I want to ask.

"Uh, I'm gonna go back to the kitchen," Gil says.

As soon as he's gone, Sara's eyes fill with tears. "I can't believe you, Mom," she says. "We weren't doing anything wrong."

"You're supposed to be working," my mom says. "Not sneaking off to make out with the busboy. What if dad caught you instead of me? Do you want to get Gil fired?"

"You kissed Gil?" I ask, surprised. I almost shudder but stop myself.

"Thanks for sharing, Mom," Sara says. "Could you ruin my life any more?"

"Oh, don't be so dramatic. Fern won't tell anyone," my mom says.

Sara eyes me.

"Why were you kissing Gil?" I ask.

Charlie makes a kissy noise.

"Shut up," Sara says.

"What did *I* do?"

My mom sighs.

"Why is it OK for you to go off and meditate all

the time, but I can't take a little break once in a while?"
Sara asks her.

I can tell that got my mom's attention by the way she presses her lips together. Like she's trying to keep from yelling.

"That's not the same thing," she says.

Sara crosses her arms. "Whatever."

"Let's just get back to work before the rush and forget the whole thing. I won't tell your father. This time."

"Um, the rush is *over*," I say. "I guess you guys were too busy kissing and meditating to notice."

"Mona can handle things," my mom snaps back.

"Like watch Charlie *and* take all the orders? What the hell, Mom? Mona can't do everything."

"Watch your tongue, Fern!"

"What channel is it on?" Charlie asks. He got that joke from Holden. I don't think he even knows what it means.

"Charlie, that's rude." She turns to me. "And I don't like your attitude."

"Well, I don't like signing autographs!" I say. "Dad's made us all famous!"

"What do you mean?" Sara asks.

"See you at Hawee's!" Charlie shouts.

Exactly.

My mom groans and glances back at the office door longingly. I swear, if she goes in there to meditate again, I will scream so loudly, her inner peace will run away for good.

Charlie and I don't follow my mom and sister back into the dining room. Instead, I take Charlie outside. There's a grassy area under a huge oak tree near the parking lot with a few picnic tables under it. It's Gil's job to wash the bird poop off the tables. This afternoon it's clear that he's been too busy hanging out with Sara.

Charlie crawls under the table with Doll and tells me I'm the Big Bad Wolf. I growl once to make him happy.

"That wolf is mean," Charlie tells Doll in a loud whisper. I know I shouldn't take it personally, but I do.

"And ugly!"

I wonder if Charlie is in range of my foot so I could "accidentally" kick him.

"That wolf's gonna eat us up," Charlie whispers.

As I start to growl again, I hear loud music and feel the bass thumping in my chest as Gray's car pulls into the parking lot. He drives over to us and rolls down his window. "Hey, Fern!" he shouts. "Where's your brother?!"

"Here!" Charlie yells, poking his head out from under the table.

"Not you," I say. "Holden."

"I haven't seen him since you guys dropped me off!" I yell to Gray.

"He needs a cell phone!" he yells back. Then he peels out of the parking lot.

"Who was that?" Charlie asks.

"That was Gray."

"He's loud." He pops his head back under the table, then slips out the other side and makes a dash for it.

"Charlie!" I scream. "No running in the parking lot!"

"You won't get me, Big Bad Wolfie!" He continues his mad dash across the pavement just as a car is backing up.

Brakes screech.

I'm running. Charlie is on his back, still clutching Doll. His face is very calm. "Wolf!" he screams up at me. But he doesn't move.

The driver gets out of the car and hurries around to the back. It's Mr. Seymore, a skinny old man who comes into the restaurant all the time for the senior-citizen early-bird discount.

"Jeee-*sus*!" he yells. "Is he OK? I don't think I hit him. I didn't feel anything."

"Charlie?" I ask. Something is happening in my chest. My heart. It's beating so fast and so hard. I have to press my hands against it. I can't breathe. I look down at Charlie, who is impossibly still.

Then he blinks.

I bend down to touch his face with my hand. "Are you hurt? Where does it hurt?"

"Can't catch me, Wolfie!" He rolls away from me and dashes toward the restaurant. "Can't catch me nevah, nevah!"

I take a deep breath. I still feel like I'm in shock.

Mr. Seymore scratches his head. "Miracle I didn't hit the kid. I could've killed 'im! You shouldn't let your little brother run in the parking lot."

"I didn't! He took off before I could grab him!"

"There are rules!" he yells in my face. He's shaking. I realize I am, too.

"He was so fast," I say.

My mom comes running out of the restaurant. "Fern! What did you do to your brother?"

I'm still having trouble breathing.

"Fern!" my mother yells.

Mr. Seymore shakes his head. "Can't believe I didn't kill the kid," he says. "Stupid kids."

My ears are buzzing.

"Fern? What's *wrong* with you?" My mom's staring at me like I'm a child killer.

I gasp for breath.

"He ... he..." I try.

Charlie darts back outside and comes careening into me. "Bad Wolf!" he says, hugging my legs like he always does.

"Did you scare him?" my mom asks.

Sara comes out then, too. "What happened?"

I touch Charlie's soggy head.

"He darted out," I say quietly. "I couldn't stop him."

My mom gives me a disappointed look.

I pull Charlie off my legs in disgust. "He's fine," I say. "Charlie, never do that again! You could've been hit!"

He head-butts my thigh. "It didn't hurt," he says, rubbing the back of his head.

My mom bends down and kisses him.

And where were you? I want to scream at her.

"He really could've been hurt, Fern," my mom says as she stands back up.

"I know that! But he's not *my* responsibility!"

"He's all of our responsibility. We're a family."

"Go, team!" Charlie cheers.

"Then do your share!" I give Sara a dirty look. "I have homework. I can't watch him all the time." I'm still shaking from seeing Charlie on the ground like that. Mr. Seymore is right. He could have killed him. But it would have been my fault. Me. The one who's supposed to save everyone.

Mr. Seymore walks away from us, muttering as he gets into his car.

Sara gives me a look like I am the worst sister on earth. Then she and my mom lead Charlie back inside. I notice they don't seem to care whether *I* was in harm's way.

I walk back to the picnic table and sit there, alone. I look at all the names carved and penned into the tabletop. Mostly there are first names with *was here* and then the year. Or else there are things like *Carrie loves Ben 4-evah*. It's kind of a tradition, I guess, to come here and carve something on the tables, because the tables have become plastered and gouged over the years, and some of the dates go back to when my grandfather first opened the business. People have even carved stuff under the table and seats because it's so hard to find free space. Holden once suggested we paint over them, and my dad was offended. He said the etchings are what give the tables character and add to the old-timey ambience of the restaurant.

As I study the carvings, I feel a hand on my shoulder and jump.

"Whoa!" Holden says, sitting down next to me. "Didn't mean to scare you."

"Where've you been? I ask. "Gray was looking for you."

"He found me. We going home soon?"

"I dunno."

"What's wrong?"

"Charlie almost got hit by a car, and everyone thinks it's my fault."

"Is he OK?"

"Yeah," I say quietly.

"So, *was* it your fault?"

"No! Charlie was playing under the table and then

just took off and ran across the parking lot before I could stop him. I was trying to do my homework. Mom's the one who's supposed to be taking care of him, not me."

"Well..."

"Don't even think about telling me we're a team."

"OK." He traces his finger along one of the bigger names carved on the tabletop. Then he pulls out the mini Swiss Army knife on his key chain and starts carving teeny-tiny letters inside a peace sign someone else made. I watch while he carefully carves out the almost unreadable words. *Holden was here*. Then he hands the knife to me.

"What am I supposed to do with this?"

"Be creative."

I slide closer to him and carefully push the tip of the knife into the wood and try to form letters under Holden's. *Fern 2*.

"What are you doing to that table?"

I jump for a second time and almost cut myself.

My mom is walking toward us. Charlie and Sara trail behind.

"Marking our territory," Holden tells her.

"Me, too!" Charlie yells, reaching for the knife.

I push his hand away just in time.

"You mean!" He pouts at me.

I hate it when he says that. "I didn't want you to cut yourself – that's all!"

"Wite my name," he demands.

"Fine." I carefully add *& Charlie*. Charlie squeezes in between Holden and me so he can see. His small hand pushes down on my thigh as he leans forward and squints at the letters. He turns and smiles at me. Then he reaches for my ear and pulls it toward his face. I feel his warm little breath in it and cringe, wondering what he'll do.

"I love you, Ferny," he whispers. Then he leans back and giggles and kisses Doll's green hair.

"I love you, too," I say. Because just at that moment, I really do. Despite how much of a huge pain he is. Seeing him on the pavement, lying so still, I realize just how much I love him.

My mom puts her hand on Charlie's head and smiles at his cuteness. "Let's go home," she says. "It's been a long day."

16

ON THE WAY HOME, my mom tells Charlie he can have whatever he wants for dinner because she's so happy he didn't get hurt.

I try to exchange eye rolls with Holden from across the seat, but he's staring out the window with a serious look on his face.

Charlie pushes Doll into my lap. Her dress is soggy from him sucking on the hem.

"Um. Ew?" I say, pushing her back.

"Doll needs wuv!" Charlie says, shoving her back.

"Then give it to her!" I say. I block her from getting any closer.

"You do it!" Charlie says.

"No!"

"Fern, for God's sake just humour him," my mom says from the front seat.

"Make Holden do it!"

"Doll wants Fern!" Charlie whines, but he pushes Doll toward Holden, who finally comes back to earth.

"Ick," he says. "I don't want her."

"Doll's not icky!" Charlie says. He starts to cry.

"You two are awful," Sara says. "Humour the kid, Fern. You should be flattered."

"Fine." I take the stupid doll from Charlie and put her on my lap.

"Sing!" Charlie says, magically not crying anymore.

I groan and lean my head back in the seat. Luckily, we pull into the driveway before Charlie can start fake-crying again.

Inside, my mom, Sara, and Charlie go straight to the kitchen, so I follow Holden into the living room. He has an instruction booklet open on his knee, and he's pushing buttons on a cell phone.

"Hey! Where'd you get that?" I ask.

He shrugs. "Gray gave it to me."

"Wow."

"Yeah. Now he can text me and stuff. It's cool."

"So does this mean he's like, you know, officially your boyfriend or something?"

"Or something? What's that supposed to mean?"

"I dunno. I mean. Is that what you'd call him?"

Holden sighs. "Well, yeah, I guess so. I mean, I'm kind of new to all this. Gray's the first guy I've met who ... you know. Is like me."

"But you're not just friends."

"No." He smiles, as if it just sank in that he has someone special. "Anyway. What about you?"

"What about me?"

"Any hot guys in middle school you're crushing on?"

I blush. "Right."

"Fern, you're cute. You need to realize that."

I look away. "No, I'm not."

"Sure you are! But you're always hiding behind your hair and baggy clothes. It's like you try to blend in so you're invisible. Why do you do that?"

I shrug. I never thought that's what makes me invisible. I never thought the fact that I'm invisible is my fault.

He reaches over and pushes my hair back, then studies my face. "You could be really pretty, Fern. Too bad the only one who knows it is Ran."

"Ran?"

"I've seen him look at you."

My cheeks get even hotter. Ran?

"He thinks you're hot," he says, grinning.

"I'm twelve! I'm not supposed to be hot yet. You're just saying that to embarrass me."

"Fern the hottie!" he says, laughing.

"Shut up!" But I'm laughing, too.

Charlie comes dashing out to the living room with Doll tucked under his arm. "Hi!" he says, beaming. Something that I hope is chocolate pudding is all over the corners of his mouth. There's also a spot on his forehead. My mom must feel pretty bad if she gave him chocolate before dinner, even if it is that gross carob stuff and not the real thing.

"Dude, go wash your face," Holden says.

Charlie leans forward as if he's going to wipe his face on Holden's shirt.

"Hey!" Holden puts his hand on Charlie's head and pushes him back. "Yuck. Tell Mom you need a bath. Your hair is sticky."

Holden wipes his hand on his jeans.

"You mean." Charlie sulks back to the kitchen.

"That kid is disgusting," Holden says.

"I know." Everything about Charlie is dismissed as cute. Even his dirtiness. I really wish my mom would take better care of him.

Music comes from Holden's cell. He smiles at me and opens it. "Guess who?" he says.

I make a face like I can't imagine.

"He-ey," he says into the phone. He gets up and heads toward the stairs while he talks. "I know! I know! Check it out! Thanks so much!"

I stay on the couch and listen to my mom's and Sara's voices coming from the kitchen. They're singing to UB40 at the top of their lungs. Charlie must have climbed into his high chair because I can hear his legs banging to the music. Normally I would roll my eyes and feel all annoyed, but I have to admit that I'm so glad he's OK, he can bang all he wants.

At dinner, Charlie is delirious, shoving orange cheesy noodles in his mouth. My mom made what we call the "bad" mac and cheese. It's the bright orange kind from a box instead of her homemade organic. My dad came home to eat with us as a special treat, and everyone seems pretty happy for the first time in a long time. My dad tells us that he decided to go with just Charlie on the label for the ice cream. We all prod him until he finally admits that some of the ad designers thought it was more appealing than our family photo. We all think this is pretty funny. And it feels great to laugh with my dad and not hurt his feelings.

About halfway through dinner, though, Holden's new phone rings. He pulls it out and opens it to see who's calling. As if he doesn't know.

"Where did you get that?" my dad asks before Holden can answer the phone.

"A friend," he says, starting to put the phone to his ear.

My dad reaches across the table and grabs Holden's arm to stop him from answering. "Oh, no, you don't," he says. "Turn that thing off. It's dinnertime."

"But—"

"Off."

Holden frowns and closes the phone.

"Now. I'm asking again. Where did that come from?" my dad asks.

"A friend," Holden says.

"That's an awfully expensive gift, honey," my mom says.

Holden shrugs. I can see where this is headed, and I know it's not good.

"What friend?" my dad asks.

Holden looks at me as if I can help him with this one. "A school friend. Gray."

"*Gray?*" my dad asks.

"He's nice," I say.

"And old," Charlie adds.

"What the—?" Holden starts.

"Now, Charlie," my mom says at the same time.

"How old?"

No one answers.

"Would someone please tell me what's going on?" my dad asks.

No one will.

"You know what? This wouldn't even be an issue if Gray were a girl."

"Holden, that's not true," my mom says.

"Just forget it." Holden gets up and storms out of the room. A few seconds later, the front door slams.

We all sit quietly for a minute.

I watch my dad chew, mulling over everything that

just happened. I swear I can hear the cogs in his brain working, putting the pieces together.

"So, this is it," he says. "It's really true?"

My mom and Sara look at each other.

"Try not to freak out, Dad," Sara says.

"But he's so *young*. How can he know?"

"Honey," my mom says. "We've all known for ages."

My dad sighs. "I don't like this. How old is this kid, anyway?"

Sara, my mom, and I all look at each other. Finally, my mom tells him. "Don't overreact, honey. But he's a senior at the Academy. Fern says he's very nice."

"A *senior*? Good God. That's not right. He could be taking advantage of – He could – Well, I don't like this. No. This isn't—"

My dad keeps sputtering.

"Are you OK, Daddy?" Charlie asks.

"This is hard for Holden, too," I say. They all look at me. "I mean, it's a big step for him. I think we should all try to be supportive."

My dad just shakes his head. "No. No dating. He's too young."

"You let me date when I was fourteen," Sara says.

"That's different. I didn't let you date a senior! And you weren't … confused."

"Holden isn't confused," I say.

"No. No, no," my dad says. He takes a long drink from his wineglass.

"Let's talk about this later," my mom says, standing up to clear the table. "Fern, go find your brother."

Outside, the late September air is cold. Leaves crumble under my feet as I walk down the path to the road. I look down each way, but I don't see any sign of Holden.

I wander over to our neighbor's yard and our old tree. Inside, Holden is sending a text on his new cell. He stops when he sees me.

"What are you doing here?"

I shrug and sit down.

"I'm not staying. You should go home."

"Why do you keep leaving?"

"Why shouldn't I?"

I lean against the tree, even though I know I'll probably get pine pitch on my shirt. "Because we love you. No one cares if you like boys. You know that, right? It just seems like sometimes you look for an excuse to leave – that's all. Like you don't want to have anything to do with us."

"Whatever."

"Why are you mad at *me*? I didn't do anything."

"I'm not mad at you. It's just … No one gets it."

I cross my arms. The tree digs into my back, but I don't move.

"I get it," I say quietly. "I understand."

"What do you get? You think you understand what it's like? I don't think so, Fern."

"Then, tell me!"

A car beeps and Holden jumps up, hitting his head on a branch. Suddenly, he no longer fits in our cave.

"I have to go," he says.

"Whatever," I say, using his favourite word.

He stoops under the branches and lopes across our neighbor's lawn, leaving me alone. I sit forward and brush the loose pine needles on the ground into a pile like a campfire. I pick a small handful up and smell the orange needles.

There's nowhere for me to go now, and there won't be later, either. I wait as long as I can, but the night air is so cold, I finally go back home.

Charlie is upstairs in the bathtub, singing. The door is open, and when I walk by, I can see my mom sitting on the floor next to the tub, her feet propped up on the toilet. She's reading a vegetarian cooking magazine and tearing out recipes. There's a small pile on the toilet seat. At least she's sort of paying attention to Charlie while he's in the tub. Half the time she just leaves the door open while he plays in there, and I feel the need to check every two minutes to make sure he hasn't drowned. Maybe today's big scare in the parking lot has changed her.

I go to my room and check my e-mail. No new messages. How shocking. I think about calling Ran or even Cassie, but realize I don't really feel like talking to anyone. So I do my homework and read myself to sleep instead.

17

WHEN I WAKE UP, I'm covered in sweat. It's 5:14. My whole body is prickling with heat. I kick off my blankets to cool off. I stare at the ceiling and think about school and what I should wear today. I try to remember what I have that's clean. The more I think, the more awake I become, and I know I am never going to fall back to sleep. I roll over on my back and stare at the ceiling with the quiet of the house humming in my ears. For a long time, I had to share a room with Charlie. I was so upset when my parents started assembling the old crib in the corner of my room. When I asked why he couldn't sleep with my parents, they gave a lame excuse about my dad coming home late from work and not wanting to wake the baby.

Every night, Charlie would wake up crying. There was a baby monitor in the room, so my mom could hear when he woke up. She'd come in like a shadow and scoop him out of the crib. She'd nurse him while she held him in the rocking chair that took up a huge space in the corner. She'd hum quiet songs to him that helped me go back to sleep, too. I always wished she'd stop and pat my head or check on me on her way back to her room, but I always fell asleep before she finished, so I don't know if she ever did.

When Charlie stopped nursing, my mom got rid of the monitor. But Charlie still never slept through the night. I would get up when he woke and rub his back until he went back to sleep. He was a loud breather, and at first it kept me up. But after a while, I got used to it and relied on that steady rhythm to help me get to sleep at night.

Last year my parents finally agreed that I needed my privacy, and my dad moved his desk into my parents' room and gave Charlie his old office. I never admitted it to anyone, but for weeks I had trouble falling asleep in the quiet of my room. I wouldn't say I missed him, but I missed his breathing.

I close my eyes in the quiet and try to fall back to sleep, but it's no use. I finally drag myself up and take a shower. One good thing about being the first one up is a long shower with no worry about running out of hot water. By the time I'm done, it's almost six thirty. Charlie, our family alarm clock, is usually awake by now. He runs down the hallway and bangs on everyone's bedroom door as he makes his way to my parents' room. I don't like to shut my door, so usually when he gets to mine, he knocks on the door frame and calls, "Up, up, up, Ferny!" Sometimes he comes in and pokes Doll close to my face. I always know she's there before I open my eyes because I can smell her odd Doll smell. A mixture of rubber and peanut-butter crackers.

As I walk down the hallway, I pause at his room and look inside. His curly hair is sticking out from under his blankets. I think about knocking on his door and whispering, *Up, up, up, Char-Char!* but I know he'll tell my parents I woke him up and they'll be upset about missing a once-in-a-lifetime opportunity to sleep in, even if it's only an extra fifteen minutes.

After my shower, I go back to my room and gather

my stuff for school, then head downstairs. It feels so strange to be the only one up. I go to the kitchen and put an English muffin in the toaster, then pour myself some orange juice. By the time my muffin is ready, I check the clock again. It's almost seven. I can't believe I'm still the only one awake. There is definitely going to be a fight for the shower.

I put my dishes in the dishwasher and go back upstairs. The bathroom is still open, so I go in and brush my teeth. When I turn the water off, I hear the distinct sound of an angry Sara.

"Hey! Why didn't anyone wake me up!"

I step into the hallway. She's standing in the door to her bedroom.

"Charlie decided to sleep in," I say.

"And you didn't think to get me up? If you want a ride, you have to help out!"

"Sorry! I didn't—"

Holden opens his own door. "Don't even think about going in next," he says.

They both dash for the bathroom, but Holden gets in first.

"MOM!" Sara runs down the hall and slams her fist on my parents' door.

My mom finally opens it, hugging her bathrobe to her chest. "Where's Charlie?" she asks.

"He's still asleep. Fern got up but didn't bother to wake anyone else, and now we're all going to be late."

My mom sighs. "I think we'll all survive."

Wow. She didn't blame me for something. She pads down the hall to Charlie's room in her bare feet and peeks in. "It's a miracle he's sleeping through all this," she says, coming back out to the hall.

"I'm not going to be able to drive them to school," Sara says.

"Why not?"

"I haven't showered!"

"But you've taken us before without showering."

"Well, not today."

"Just relax," my mom says. "I can manage. Though why they can't take the bus I still don't understand."

Sara shoots me a look.

I follow my mom back downstairs. She gets the coffee going and starts cutting up some orange slices for Charlie's breakfast. They look good. Soon my dad comes bounding down the stairs in a T-shirt and enormous sweatpants with a gym bag. He kisses my mom on the cheek and says he'll shower at the gym. The gym is a new experience for my dad. He discovered it's a great place to give his sales pitch to local businessmen. Holden joked that seeing my dad naked in the sauna was sure to be a business turnoff, but no one but me saw the humour.

"Guess we better wake Charlie if I'm going to take you to school," my mom says, downing the rest of her coffee. I put my books in my backpack and sit in the living room to wait. I hear the water in the bathroom shut off and start again, meaning Holden is out and Sara is in.

And then I hear the strangest sound I've ever heard. It sounds like *no* and *help* at the same time. It sounds like an animal trying to speak human. It sounds like it is dying.

I stand up.

"Mom?"

I hear it again.

It's her.

I run up the stairs.

"Mom?"

Holden is in the hallway, his hair still wet.

"What was that noise?" he asks.

I run past him and stop at the door to Charlie's room.

My mom is on Charlie's bed, rocking him.

"What's wrong?" I ask. But already I can feel something. Something squeezing my heart into a stone. Charlie doesn't look right. He's gray and still. His brown curls hang dully over my mom's arm. Her face is buried in his hair. She's saying something, but I can't make out the words.

"Oh, my God," Holden says behind me. "I'm calling 911." He runs back down the hall.

I don't move. I just stare at my mom holding Charlie. Rocking him and making that strange, awful noise.

The water in the shower stops. Holden's voice is back in the hallway. "Sara, get out here! Something's wrong with Charlie!"

He pushes past me and runs to my mom and Charlie, but stops when he touches him and pulls his hand away.

"Oh, my God," he says. "Oh, my God! Oh, my God!"

My mom is sobbing into Charlie's head.

My heart is twisting, twisting, twisting inside my chest and up into my throat. I can't move. I can't move.

Sara comes up behind me wrapped in a towel.

"What's going on?"

Holden stands up and staggers as if he's lost his balance. I hold on to the door frame to keep myself from falling. Sara rushes to my mom and Charlie and has the same reaction as Holden. She collapses at my mom's feet and puts her arms around Charlie and my mom, as if she is holding them together.

"He's so cold," she sobs.

"Oh my God, oh my God," Holden keeps saying.

"Mom!" Sara yells.

But my mom doesn't respond. She just cries harder into Charlie's quiet face.

"Call 911!" Sara yells at me. "Don't just stand there!"

"I already called," Holden says quietly, just as we begin to hear sirens in the distance.

Sara looks back at my mom and Charlie.

She touches him again, sobbing. "No! No!'

I know what it means.

Holden moves past us and goes down the stairs. We hear his panicked voice shouting to someone outside. Then the thud of heavy feet coming through the house and up the stairs. Someone pulls me back out of the doorway. I lean against the wall in the hall, and I realize

I still have my backpack on. I slip it off and slide to the floor. I can't feel anything but my twisted-up heart, squeezing, squeezing. Everything around me is loud and pounding. My mom is sobbing. Then screaming. Then sobbing. Soothing voices from the EMTs. Questions. I hug my knees to my chest.

Charlie. Oh, Charlie. Please be OK.

But the more time goes by, the quieter the voices get. And I know. I know he's gone. As my mother's cries turn to whimpers, I can't stand it anymore.

I get up.

And I run.

18

I RUN WITHOUT THINKING where I'm going. Halfway to nowhere I stop and throw up. Up and up and up, as if my heart is coming up out of my chest. Up and up until I am doubled over and hurling in pain but not crying. Not crying.

Not crying because that would mean …

That would mean …

I wipe my mouth with my sleeve and find my way to the pine cave. But instead of going under, I start to pull on the branches. I break one, then two. I kick the trunk and feel the pain sear through my leg and up to my stomach. But then a numbness takes over. And there's a ringing in my ears. *No no no no no.*

I push the palms of my hands against my ears to shut it out. The lights from the ambulance in the driveway flash on and on. I close my eyes and finally sink down onto the cold ground. Pine needles stick to the palms of my hands. I squeeze my knees to my chest and make myself a stone, but I can't escape myself. Can't escape the truth creeping into my chest where my heart used to be. I keep shaking my head against it, but the truth is filling me up so fast I can't breathe.

There's a beeping sound as the ambulance backs up. I can see Holden and Sara standing in the driveway, watching them take Charlie away.

I listen to the motor get farther away until it's gone, and the door to the house slams shut, and the neighborhood goes from quiet to busy as the commuters leave home for another workday. I hear the school bus stop in the distance and pull away again.

And then, after a long, long time, I hear someone calling my name.

19

HOLDEN'S FEET APPEAR near a broken branch. His shoes aren't tied.

"Fern," he finally says. "You have to come home."

But I don't move.

"Fern. Now."

His knees bend, and then his face pokes in. It's swollen from crying.

"Come on."

But it takes his hand reaching for mine and pulling me out to get me to move.

When we reach the front door, he lets go of my hand.

"They said they think it was something called an epidural hematoma," he says quietly. "Some kind of blood clot in his brain or … I don't know. They don't think he felt any pain."

And he walks into the house, leaving me on the doorstep.

I don't know what an epidural hema-whatever is. All I can picture is Charlie. Charlie in his bed this morning, the covers pulled up so all I could see was his curly hair. And Doll, sitting on the pillow next to his head, where she always keeps watch.

Stepping inside the house feels like walking into darkness. Holden and Sara are both sitting on the couch. Holden stares at the coffee table. Sara is crying into a pillow. I slowly walk to the empty oversize armchair that only my mom sits in, usually with Charlie curled up in her lap. When I sink into the chair, I feel myself waiting for him to come tearing into the room. "That's Mommy's chair!" he would yell, then crawl into my lap and pretend I was Mom. I close my eyes and wait for him to come. Wait for his sharp baby voice. For the brush of his stinky hair on my face. For the smell of Doll as he makes room for her next to me. For the feel of his pudgy hands squeezing my wrist.

And his voice, "Read to me, Ferny. I love you, Ferny," as he snuggles his head into my neck and reaches for my ear.

I wait and wait. But my lap stays empty.

Everything is empty.

20

LATER, THE FRONT DOOR OPENS, and my dad and mom walk in. My dad has his arm around my mom's waist. Sara and Holden both stand up to go to her, but my dad waves them off and leads her through the living room and up the stairs. When he comes back down, he sits next to Holden and puts his hand on his knee. He breathes in and opens his mouth as if he's about to speak, but nothing comes out. Sara moves closer to him and leans into his side. He puts his free arm around her and makes a choking sound.

Sara lifts her head and looks at my dad. "Why?" she asks.

My dad shakes his head. His voice is so quiet, it's like a whisper. "They think that whatever happened is related to when he fell yesterday."

Flashes of Charlie lying so still on the pavement flick through my mind. How he looked up at me through his tears. But then he jumped right up! He was fine!

"They think he must have hit the back of his head," my dad says. "And it caused a blood clot that went to his brain. If ... If we had just taken him to the hospital yesterday ... Maybe ... Oh God..."

Holden looks at me. "How hard did he fall, Fern?"

Sara and my dad are looking at me now, too.

The Big Bad Wolf.

"He..." I start to say. "I didn't see..." My face starts to burn. I can feel them accusing me. I let him run in the parking lot. It's all my fault.

"He was OK!" I say desperately. "He got right up! He ran! He – he wasn't even hurt!"

"Then *why*? How could this happen?" Holden stands up and starts pacing, pressing his fingers against his temples.

"They said these kinds of injuries are some sort of fluke," my dad explains. "The brain can hit against the skull just the wrong way and cause a concussion. Or something."

"I didn't know he was going to run!" I yell. "I didn't know he was playing a game with me! He just took off!"

They all stare at me.

My body is tingling all over. I feel like I am turning inside out.

"We know, Fern," my dad says. "It's not your fault."

"He just ran away from me! I didn't know what he was doing!"

Sara starts to cry again.

"He and Doll were playing! I was just doing my homework!" I yell louder because Sara won't look at me, and I know that must mean she blames me. "Mom should've taken him to the hospital! He should've had X-rays! Charlie never complains when he's hurt. Mom should have known!" I choke on the unforgivable words.

"Shut up!" Sara screams, finally facing me. "Shut up, shut up, shut up!"

"Stop it!" Holden yells. "It's no one's fault!" He pulls at his hair, then looks up at the ceiling. Up where my parents' room is. Where my mom is.

My dad reaches out and takes Holden's hand. Sara hides her face against his shoulder again. And I still sit alone.

"Come here, Fern," my dad says quietly. "It's no one's fault."

But I just shake my head and pull my knees to my chest so I can hide my own face. *No*, I keep thinking. *No*.

21

AFTER A WHILE, my dad gets up and goes to the kitchen. I imagine him coming back with a huge smile on his face saying he called the hospital and it was all just a big mistake. But instead, he comes back carrying the anniversary tray. It has a glass of water, a plate with toast, and a bottle of pills.

"I need to bring this up to your mom, but I'll be back," he says. As we watch him slowly climb the stairs, I remember all the anniversaries the three of us – and then Charlie, too – quietly climbed the stairs with that same tray, stacked with special treats for my parents. We'd knock on the door and say in our exaggerated lovey-dovey voices, "Room service!" and then giggle as we'd run down the hall and back downstairs to watch hours of bad TV that we normally weren't allowed to watch.

When Charlie was born, as a joke we left him in his bouncy seat asleep next to the tray of food in the hall. It was Holden's idea to remind my parents to be a bit more careful celebrating their anniversary that time around so we wouldn't have *another* unexpected surprise. Sara thought that was crude, but I thought it was pretty funny, once Holden explained the joke to me. Unfortunately, Charlie woke up before my parents retrieved their tray, so we had to go get him. Holden wanted to leave a dirty diaper in the baby seat instead, but Sara put her foot down.

While my dad's upstairs, we sit and stare. We don't look at each other. We just wait and wait. I imagine my dad giving my mom those pills. I guess they must make her sleep. I wish we could all take them.

When my dad finally comes back downstairs with the empty tray, his eyes are red and his cheeks are shiny with tears. It seems to take all his effort to walk down the final steps and sit on the couch between Holden and Sara. He pulls them to him on either side and sobs. They bury their faces in his chest and cry, too.

"Fern," he whispers. "Come here."

I look into my dad's watery, bloodshot eyes and stay where I am. I know I'm supposed to be crying. But I won't. I won't if it means what they've already accepted.

Holden gets up and walks over to me. He pries my hand from the armrest and pulls me up. I try to pull back.

"No!" I yell.

But now my dad is at my side, too. His strong arms pull me up and hold me close around his huge, soft belly. As he presses me into him, I feel like I could disappear.

I feel like I am breaking.

22

THAT NIGHT, Holden and Sara both go to their rooms to sleep, but I stay in the chair. My dad tries to carry me upstairs after I fall asleep, but I wake up and make him put me down. After he leaves me, I curl up in the chair and wait. But Charlie doesn't come back.

In the morning, my dad makes us a breakfast we don't eat, then goes upstairs to check on my mom. We still haven't seen her since she came home. I don't understand why she doesn't come down and hold us. I don't understand why we can't go up and crawl into bed with her. My dad says we need to give her some time. But I need her now.

"I have to get out of here," Holden tells Sara and me.

"Where will you go?" Sara asks.

"I just need some fresh air." But as he turns to go, the phone rings. We all look at each other.

"What do we do?" Sara asks.

"Take it off the hook," Holden says.

Before anyone can get to the phone in the kitchen, though, we hear the machine pick up, and Charlie's voice echoes through the quiet house. "Hel-lo. Mom-my, Dad-dy, Sa-wuh, Hold-en, Fern, and Chah-lie ah not at home to take yo-uh call. Please leave a mes-sage, and we will call you back as soon as poss-ih-bull. Thank you. And see you at Hawee's!"

No one moves.

Beeeeeep.

"Hello? Is anyone there? It's Mona. Oh, God, we just heard. Um. Oh. Um. Please call when you can. We're all here. Um. OK. We'll try to call again later."

Beeeeep.

"I'll turn it off," Holden says quietly.

I pull my knees to my chest again as he walks away.

"Fern," Sara says. "Fern, you have to stop doing that. It's OK to cry."

I shake my head and tuck my face between my knees again.

"Fern," Sara says. She touches the top of my head.

"Stop!" I yell at her. "Stop! I don't want to … to … Just stop!"

"Stop what?" she asks quietly.

"Stop acting like he's … like he's not coming back."

Sara kneels in front of me and wraps her arms around my legs, squeezing.

"Fern," she says again, crying, hiding her face against me.

"I should have paid more attention to him," I say. "I should have played with him. Then I wouldn't have been the Big Bad Wolf. And then—"

"It's not your fault," she says quietly.

"He was so lonely," I say.

"No, he wasn't. He was just bored."

"But if I had stopped doing my homework, maybe he wouldn't have run away from me."

"And maybe if the waitress service had been better, Mr. Seymore would have left the restaurant earlier and Charlie wouldn't have run behind him. Maybe if Mom and I had come out to help sooner..." She trails off and looks away. And then she starts to cry uncontrollably. Shaking. This time I put my hand on her back, but she shrugs it off. When she finally stops, she takes a deep breath and shakes her head. "No," she says quietly. "No." She turns back to me. "It was an accident. Do you understand? It wasn't your fault. It was—" But she stops and turns away again, as if she can't lie to my face. As if it's too hard to convince me.

"I'll be home in a little while," Holden says, coming from the kitchen. "I took the phone off the hook." He pauses in front of the door, a guilty look on his face. "I just need to get out of this house," he says. I can tell from the way he says it that he knows he shouldn't. But he leaves anyway.

Sara pulls herself up and motions for me to move over. I slide over to make room, and she sits snug against me.

"Cry, Fern," she says. "Cry right here." She pats her chest, and I rest my head against her. She puts her arms around me so tightly, I know I won't slip away. I feel my heart untwisting just a little, as if it is uncurling enough to call out for Charlie. But it doesn't find him.

"Cry," she says, and rubs my back the way my mom used to. "Please."

I unclench my hands and reach for hers. I hold on to her as tightly as I can.

If I cry, he won't come back.

I squeeze tighter.

I feel my body start to shake.

He won't come back.

"Cry," she says again, as if she needs me to.

I'm holding her so tightly, I feel my fingernails dig into her skin. The place in my chest where my heart must be hurts so badly, I know now that my grandfather probably did die from a broken heart. And I feel like I will, too.

He isn't coming back.

"I have you, Fern."

And then a sound comes out of me. And my chest opens up again, and I am holding on to Sara as I sob so hard, I think I will turn inside out. I sob and sob, and she does, too. I soak her shirt with my tears, and she soaks my hair with hers. And she holds me and holds me and doesn't get up. And eventually we tire ourselves out so much we fall asleep.

The doorbell wakes us up.

We're slightly stuck to each other, and by the time we get up, my dad is coming down the stairs. We hear him open the door and step outside. After a few minutes, he comes back in.

"That was Mona," he says. "She said she tried to call."

Sara nods. "We let the machine pick it up."

"Where's Holden?"

"He went for a walk," I say.

"If I make lunch, will anyone eat it?"

We shake our heads. He nods. And we sit there in silence. No one seems to know what we're supposed to do now. How can we do anything?

Sticking out from under the coffee table, I see a tiny plastic firefighter lying on his back, smiling up at us. I start to picture all the pieces of Charlie in the house. The half-drunk cup of milk from Charlie's dinner the night before, still waiting for him in the refrigerator. Who would throw it out? By the front door, Charlie's tiny sneakers are still lined up next to mine. His coat is on the coat hook. There's nowhere in the house that you can't see a trace of him. He is with us forever and gone forever all at once.

When Holden gets back, my dad decides to make us

lunch after all, but we barely eat. We clean up, then sit on the couch again. Every so often, my dad goes upstairs to check on my mom or answer the doorbell to receive condolences from friends. But he doesn't invite anyone in.

I wish my mom would come down and check on us. My dad keeps saying she'll be down soon. But when?

I know it doesn't make sense, but it feels like she disappeared with Charlie. And the more she stays up there, the more it feels like she isn't coming back, either. That night, Holden and Sara try to get me to come upstairs to go to sleep, but I don't want to. I don't want to feel the empty corner where Charlie used to lull me to sleep with his steady breathing.

My dad comes over and puts his hand on my head. "Come on up, honey. You shouldn't stay alone down here again."

"I'll be OK," I say quietly, staring at the firefighter.

He sighs in a worried way. "Just for tonight, then."

"I'll bring you a blanket and pillow," Sara says.

Later, wrapped in the blanket in the big chair, I wait for my eyes to adjust to the dark. I reach down and pick up the firefighter and hold him close. I trace his plastic body with my finger. There are dried bits of something on his stomach, as if he had a messy meal. I imagine it was soggy Cheerios from Charlie's fingers. But instead of disgusting me, I hold it against my heart and close my eyes so I can see Charlie. Charlie singing in the bathtub. Charlie banging his legs in his too-small high chair. Charlie pushing Doll in my face, insisting I give her a good-night kiss. Charlie.

Charlie.

Charlie.

23

THE NEXT MORNING, I wake up to the sound of coffee beans grinding. Sara, Holden, and my dad are already in the kitchen. My dad pours a tiny bit in a mug for me and fills the rest with milk, then lots of sugar. My mom doesn't like it when I drink coffee, but my dad says it will grow hair on my chest. Charlie always thought that was so funny.

I put my cup down and glance over at the refrigerator. It's covered with Charlie's magnetic letters.

My dad clears his throat and looks at each of us. He opens his mouth, but it takes a long time for him to form any words. Finally, he says, "I'm going over to the restaurant today to talk to the staff. I – I'll need them to help me make ... Arrangements. Your mom. She can't—" He grips his coffee cup. "Will you guys be OK if I leave?"

"Sure, Dad," Sara says, putting her hand on his back.

I nod, looking inside my own cup.

He finishes his coffee and puts the mug in the sink. Then he hugs each of us. When he gets to me, his huge belly squishes against my chest. His plaid wool shirt scratches my face, and I close my eyes and try to hide in it. He squeezes me extra hard before he lets go, then leaves us in the kitchen.

Holden pulls out his phone as he walks out of the room. I turn to Sara, who glances over at the phone on the wall.

"There are so many people we're going to have to tell," she says. "I don't know how that works. I can't imagine any of us doing it, you know?"

I nod. "Maybe Mona could do it. We could give her Mom's address book."

"That's a good idea. Let me see if I can catch Dad." She runs outside to wave him down, leaving me alone.

I walk over to the answering machine and stare at the flashing numbers showing all the messages we have. I remember helping Charlie record a new message just the other day. He made messages practically every week. Slowly, I press the PLAY button.

There's a fumbling noise, then the faint sound of me whispering, "OK, now."

And then Charlie in his little robot voice. "Hel-lo. Mom-my, Dad-dy, Sa-wuh, Hold-en, Fern, and Chah-lie ah not at home to take yo-uh call. Please leave a mes-sage, and we will call you back as soon as poss-ih-bull. Thank you. And see you at Hawee's!"

I put my hand on the machine, as if I am touch-ing Charlie. I lift it to my face. I play it again. "Hel-lo. Mom-my, Dad-dy, Sa-wuh, Hold-en, Fern, and Chah-lie ah not at home to take yo-uh call. Please leave a mes-sage, and we will call you back as soon as poss-ih-bull. Thank you. And see you at Hawee's!" And again. "Hel-lo. Mom-my, Dad-dy, Sa-wuh, Hold-en, Fern, and Chah-lie ah not at home to take yo-uh call. Please leave a mes-sage, and we will call you back as soon as poss-ih-bull. Thank you. And see you at Hawee's!"

His voice vibrates against my wet cheek as I play it over and over. Finally, I unplug the machine and carry it to the hall where my backpack is. I unzip my pack and hide the machine inside just as the front door opens. "Caught him," Sara says, out of breath. "I'll go get the book."

When she comes back a second time, she tells me she's going to try to get Mom up and out of bed. I want to tell her that shouldn't be her job. I want to tell her I'm scared that it is. But I don't say anything, because I think she already knows.

While Sara is upstairs, I slowly walk around the house, gathering up Charlie's toys and things. I move his high chair into the kitchen closet and put his shoes and coat in the closet in the hall. I find whatever toys and books are lying around and put them all in the antique trunk we use to hide them in when guests come over. Each time I touch something of Charlie's, I can see it in his small hands. I can see his beaming face looking up at me, begging me to play with him. And it hurts. It hurts so much. But I keep going.

Holden finds me in the living room and asks what I'm doing, but I don't know how to answer. I just know that every time I see one of Charlie's toys, it's as if it's waiting for him to come back. And every time I hold one, the ache in my chest hurts even more.

"I don't know," I say. "It's just too hard to—"

"Let me help you," he says.

Together, we quietly finish gathering Charlie's things, then sit on the couch. The water is running upstairs, so I guess Sara got my mom out of bed and into the shower. When the doorbell rings, neither of us moves to answer. It rings again.

"We should see who it is," Holden says. But neither of us gets up.

A minute later, the door creaks open and Ran walks in.

24

"I TRIED TO CALL," Ran says. "But no one answered."

For the first time, I can't read his face. I've never seen this Ran before. Usually his face matches his T-shirt motto. But today his coat is zipped up, just like his expression. And I don't know what to say.

"There was a story on the news last night," Ran says. "I didn't want to believe it. When you didn't answer the phone, I went to the restaurant this morning and saw your dad, and he ... he told me what happened. I just ... can't believe it."

When he looks at me, I wonder what he must see, because suddenly his blank expression changes and he looks exactly like how I feel. And when I see him, tears start to slip down my cheeks again, stinging the raw skin there. And then he starts to cry, too. Holden moves over on the couch so Ran can sit down. Then he pulls us both to him and we cry into his chest, our foreheads touching. I can feel Holden's heartbeat against my cheek, and I close my eyes, concentrating on the sureness of it. Grateful for it. But then the stairs creak, and we sit up and quickly wipe our faces as my mom's feet appear at the top step. We wait quietly as she starts to come down, my sister following. I realize, when I see her feet, how much I really need her. How much I want her to hold me. To tell me – I'm not sure what. Maybe just to let me know she's here. That she always will be. But when she reaches the landing, she stops and turns. "I just can't," she says. "Oh, God. Oh, God." She starts to sob. Then her feet slowly climb back up the stairs and disappear.

Holden takes a deep breath and stands up. "I need to take a walk. You guys wanna come?"

We nod.

Outside, it's chilly but sunny. We stand at the end of

the driveway and look around. Everything feels quieter. Holden kicks a stone across the road. I realize it's a school day and Ran has skipped. He shoots a stone across the road perfectly. The dog across the street comes bounding over and starts yipping at us hopefully, but he's trapped as usual.

Holden's cell rings, and he pulls it out of his pocket, turning his back to us.

"Hi," he says quietly. "Yeah... Really? Yeah. I'm here. I'm at the end of the driveway, actually... OK. OK, thanks."

He puts his phone back in his pocket.

"Gray's coming to get me," he says.

The three of us continue to quietly kick at stones until Gray's car pulls up and Holden climbs in and they drive away.

Ran looks cold and uncomfortable with his hands stuffed in his pockets.

"Come on," I say.

He follows me to the neighbors' yard and what's left of the pine-tree cave. We climb under and sit up against the tree, our arms pressed against each other.

For a long time, we don't talk. I can feel our thoughts swirling together. Our memories. Our emptiness.

"When my mom was sick, I used to imagine what it would be like if she died," he says after a while. "I used to ask my dad what would happen to us. But he would just shake his head and not answer. He'd already lost his job because he kept staying home to take care of her. I kind of had to take care of myself, even though I didn't really know how."

I picture Ran when I first knew him. With his too-small clothes and always-runny nose.

"Anyway, one weekend, I went and stayed with my grandma, and she took me to her church. The minister told a story about this mystic who believed that even when there was all this horrible stuff going on, like the plague, that all would be well. She had this chant, and no matter how horrible things got, she would keep saying it. *All will be well,* she'd say. *All will be well, and all will be well, and all manner of things will be well.* The minister had everyone in church say the chant, too. And I remember sitting there, hearing everyone around me say those words, and I started to believe them. So after church, I started saying them to myself. Muttering them every time I got scared about my mom. And pretty soon she got better. And I really believed it was because of my chanting. So I kept doing it. And life just kept getting better. My parents started the T-shirt company together. Business boomed. I really thought if you said the words and believed them, they would be true."

He stops for a minute and takes a sad, deep breath. I do the same and smell the piney Christmas smell and realize that Christmas will never be the same again.

"But the whole thing was a scam," Ran says. "It was just some stupid thing to say to make me believe life isn't unfair. And just when I thought life was perfect, it became unbearable again."

I think of all the times Ran has said those words to me. He said them like they were a fact. I always secretly loved when he said them because I thought if anyone knew how things were going to turn out, it would be Ran.

"I was so wrong," he says quietly. "I'm sorry, Fern."

The ache in my throat throbs harder, but I don't cry again. I breathe in the cold air and concentrate on the branches in front of me. The hundreds of needles poking out of each thin stick. I think of all the times Holden and I hid under here, listening to Charlie call out for us. "Holdy and Ferny! Whe-ah ah you!" How we giggled and shushed each other so he wouldn't find us.

Why didn't we want him to find us?

My mom said she named me Fern because she knew I was going to be a good friend. That I was the kind of person who would save anyone in trouble. But she was wrong. I couldn't save anyone. I didn't even try.

"I wish he knew how much I love him," I say quietly. "But I was always telling him to leave me alone. What if he thinks I didn't love him?"

"He knew – knows," Ran says. He reaches for my hand and holds it gently. "He knows."

When the sun moves and leaves us in the shade, we both start to shiver.

"I should probably go," Ran says.

We climb out of the cave and walk back to my yard. The house seems quiet. We both look up at the front door but stay standing outside. Charlie's tricycle is tipped over next to the garage. I think we notice it at the same time because we both turn away. Usually when Ran goes home, he leaves me with some sort of slogan that matches whatever T-shirt he's wearing. Today he just looks at me with sad eyes I've never seen before.

Help me, I say with my own eyes.

But his say back, *I can't.*

25

THAT NIGHT AT DINNER, my dad tells us about the plans he's made for the funeral. And Charlie's ashes. He chokes on the words, but the rest of us are all cried out. We stare at our plates and listen to him, but we don't answer. My mom is still upstairs. My dad tells us he will get her to come down tomorrow. But I want her now. I want her to be the one to hold me, not Sara. I want her to tell me it's OK to cry. I want her to show us that she isn't going to disappear, too.

Instead, my dad has to tell us about funeral plans and ashes and how we'll have to decide as a family what we'll do with them. My grandparents' ashes were scattered in the lake where they both loved to sail when they were young. But where would Charlie's go? He would be all alone.

And then I remember.

"Doll!" I yell, standing up.

Everyone looks at me like I'm crazy.

"Charlie can't be … He needs Doll! Are we too late, Dad?"

My dad looks totally confused.

"Calm down, Fern. What are you talking about?"

"Charlie and Doll! They should be together!"

Sara and Holden exchange looks. "She's right," Sara says.

"Can we get her to him?" The familiar ache in my chest starts to push up my throat again.

"I … I don't know," my dad says.

"Please! We have to!"

"I'll try, Fern. I'll bring her first thing in the morning."

"Promise! You can't just try!"

"I promise," he says quietly.

I feel bad for making him go back to wherever it is he has to go, but I would feel worse if Charlie was alone.

"I'm sorry, Dad," I say. "But—"

"I know, Fern. It's OK."

That really puts an end to dinner, so we all clear our plates and clean up.

I want to sleep in the living room again, but my dad says I need to get a real night's sleep in my own room. When everyone goes upstairs, I get my backpack from the front closet and bring it to my room.

After brushing my teeth, I step into the dark hallway. No one has turned on the night-light that we keep on outside Charlie's room. I can see well enough to find it and turn it on. It's in the shape of Snoopy's doghouse. It was Sara's when she was little, then Holden's, then mine, and finally Charlie's. A faded Snoopy lies asleep on top. Charlie used to sit on the floor in the hall and pet Snoopy's belly as he told him to have sweet dreams.

I sit on the floor and touch the plastic. I feel it get warm from the heat of the lightbulb inside.

"Fern?" Sara whispers. I turn. She makes her way to the bathroom. "What are you doing?"

I don't know.

"Get some sleep," she says before she disappears inside.

I stand up and look down the hallway. Charlie's room

is on the left; mine is on the right, just beyond. The hallway is so quiet, it echoes in my ears. I'm used to Charlie's quiet snores or the steady scritch-scratch of his fingers on the wall as he talks himself to sleep, telling Doll stories.

I strain to listen. It's so quiet, it hurts. I cover my ears and hurry to my dark room. I shut my door, grab my backpack, and pull out the answering machine. I plug it in and crawl into bed, pulling the covers over me and the machine. I turn the volume down as low as it can go, then press PLAY and slowly turn the volume up so I can just barely hear. Hear Charlie. I hold my hand on the speaker and feel his voice gently vibrate against my palm.

"See you at Hawee's," he lies happily. I rewind the tape and play the broken promise again. And again. I will never see him again. I will never see his tiny hand waving to me through the glass. Or Doll's face, bobbing up and down excitedly, as if she's been waiting for me all day. I let the words fill the empty space inside me that aches and aches. But every time the machine goes quiet, I feel the emptiness open up again. I breathe in and out through my mouth to fill the quiet. In. Out. Over and over. Until I fall asleep.

26

THE NEXT MORNING, when I step into the hallway, the light in Charlie's room is on and I can hear a sobbing sound coming from inside. I step back into the shadow of my room. After a few minutes, I see my dad come out of Charlie's room with Doll in his hands. He pauses outside the door and wipes his eyes with the cuffs of his shirt. I listen to him go down the stairs before I crawl back into bed.

When my dad comes back home, he tells us all to eat breakfast and then get some warm clothes on. "We're getting out of here for a bit," he says.

When we're heading down the driveway, Sara asks where we're going. No one mentions that my mom still hasn't left her bedroom.

"Away from the house. Just for a little while," my dad says.

We drive through town and back out the other side, along the lake. It's a cold late-September day, so no one is at the beach. My dad parks in the empty lot, and we all get out. He gets the thick wool picnic blanket from the back and leads us to the far end of the beach, out of sight of the parking lot. We sit along the edge of the blanket, facing the water. The wind is blowing, causing small whitecaps on the waves. We sit there listening to the steady lap of the water on the shore. We've been here as a family so many times. My dad used to throw us up out of the water so we could cannonball one another. He taught us how to float on our backs and look up at the clouds. And Holden and I used to dig holes in the sand to make a swimming pool for Doll.

A group of seagulls nears. In their screechy chatter, I can almost hear the echo of Charlie's giggles.

The ache in my chest rises up in my throat again. I want to scream at the birds, at the water, at the sky. *It isn't fair!*

It isn't fair.

My dad gets up and walks to the edge of the water. He picks up a stone and skips it out across the surface. It hops three times before it disappears. We watch him silently from the blanket. The cold air blows between us. Even though I am sitting between my brother and sister, I feel more alone than I've ever felt in my whole life. I close my eyes and will Charlie to come running up behind me, put his sticky hands over my eyes, and scream, "Guess who?" in my ear. I wait and wait.

My dad comes back over to us and kneels in the sand, facing us. His hair is all windblown, and I think it looks grayer. He looks down at his giant thighs and rubs his hands on them.

"I made arrangements for the memorial service to be on Sunday afternoon." He turns away and looks at the lake. "And on Monday, Fern and Holden, you'll go back to school. Sara, Mom, and I will go back to work at the restaurant. I think … I think we need to get back into a routine. The sooner, the better."

"Mom can't even get out of bed," Holden says.

My dad sighs. "She will."

But how does he know? How does he know she'll come down? How does he know she won't stay up there forever? How does he know she won't just fade away?

We're all quiet again. So quiet I can't stand it. A seagull comes over and dips its head toward my dad's leg. He shoos it off. If Charlie were here, he'd chase it away with Doll, giggling as he ran.

I want him back.

I want him to come running up the beach and scream, "Surprise! I'm OK! It was all a big mistake!"

But the beach stays deserted, except for us.

"It's my fault," I whisper. "If I'd caught up to him fast enough, I could've pushed him out of the way." I imagine myself shoving Charlie aside just in time. I imagine me being the one to fall on the pavement. *Got you, Big Bad Wolf!* Charlie would say, laughing. And I would be the hero. Fern. The one who saves.

"It should have been me."

"Don't, Fern," Holden says.

But I imagine how different everything would be. If it had been me, everyone would have Charlie to make them feel better. And me being gone wouldn't really feel all that different, since no one really notices me anyway. It would have been so much *better* if it had been me instead.

"It's true. I was the Big Bad Wolf. He ran away from me because I wasn't paying attention to him. I was ignoring him!"

"Don't do this, honey," my dad says. He puts his warm hand on my shoulder, but I shrug it off.

"You know it's true! " I yell. "All he wanted was a little attention. But I just ignored him! It's all my fault!"

"Stop it!" Sara screams. And we all turn to look at her. "Stop saying that! Stop thinking it!" She's scratched her face. "I can't stand it!" she yells. "Just stop!"

But I can't. Because I know it's true.

I get up and run to the water. I don't know what I'm thinking, but I just start walking in. The truth feels like it's crushing me. Drowning me before I even get up to my knees.

The water seeps through my sneakers and up my jeans. It's icy cold, and it's such a relief to feel an outside hurt take over the hurt inside. The pain stings my ankles and crawls up my legs as I walk in deeper.

"Fern!" they all call behind me, but I don't turn. I walk in deeper. I slam my fists at the water. At the seagulls. At the sky.

"Why did you do it! He was just a little boy!" I scream and splash and shake from the cold. All the while I can see Charlie in my mind. Hear him laughing. See him looking back at me as he ran away. Me. The Big Bad Wolf coming to get him.

I slam my fists into the water again, stepping in deeper.

"I need him back!" I scream. "Give him back!" I push myself forward into more cold. It takes my breath away and I am choking. "Please give him back!"

Strong hands grab my shoulders and pull me toward the shore.

"No! No!" I scream, trying to break free. "Let me go!" I swing my fists.

The arms fold around me.

"I can't! I can't!" I scream. "I can't!"

I can't live. I can't act like life can keep going on without him. That all will be well. It won't! Nothing will ever be right again. Nothing.

"It's OK. It's OK now. Let it out." My dad's voice is quiet and calm in my ear.

But there is nothing to let out.

Nothing.

I am empty.

He wraps me in the blanket and buckles me in the backseat, and we all drive back home. Sara guides me to the upstairs bathroom and runs a hot bath for me, then leaves me alone. I undress and pull back the shower curtain. I already put Charlie's bath toys under the sink, but there are still traces of him here. Fingerprints of bathtub paint that haven't dissolved with the water yet. I touch them, careful not to smudge them in any way. I can feel the panic rising in my chest again, but I swallow it back down. I pour the bubble bath Charlie loved in the water and swish it around. It smells like Charlie when he first comes out of the bath and runs around naked from room to room, a devilish grin on his face as he shakes his bare bottom at us and runs off again with naked Doll dangling from one hand.

I put my soap-covered hands to my face and cry again. Cry and cry until I get so used to the smell I can't smell it anymore, and I have to open the bottle and breathe it in. Breath after breath after breath.

27

THE DAY BEFORE THE FUNERAL, my mom finally comes downstairs. She's wearing my dad's sweats, and her hair is stringy and gross. She stands at the kitchen counter and holds herself up by leaning on her elbow against the counter. My dad gives her a cup of coffee, and she sips it quietly. Her face is grayish, and her eyes seem sunken in.

She doesn't look like our mom. She looks like a ghost of her.

I had hoped when she came down, she would wrap us up in her arms like she used to do with Charlie.

And she would tell us she was here, just like when she'd come into my room at night when I woke up from a nightmare. "I'm here," she'd whisper. "I'm here." Until I fell back to sleep. But now I think those arms would pass right through me. It makes me feel as empty as she looks.

When she finishes her coffee, we follow her out to the living room to wait for the minister, who is stopping by to talk to us about Charlie and what will happen at the memorial service. We don't belong to a church, so Mona recommended him.

My dad greets him at the door and they talk quietly for a minute, then they come to talk with us. The minister is huge like my dad but quieter. Calmer. I wonder how many times he's had to come to a house like ours. To say words no one wants to hear.

The whole time, my parents sit on the couch and stare at the coffee table. Sara and I are squeezed into my mom's chair, and Holden stands behind us. The minister's eyes dart from one of us to another as he talks. It seems like he's been trained to do this. To make eye contact with everyone in the room. Each time our eyes meet, I feel like he can see inside me. Like he can see my guilt. I'm glad when he leaves.

All day, people stop by with casserole dishes for the service tomorrow. My dad stands in the doorway to accept them.

I'm so sorry. We're so sorry.

We hear the words over and over through the open door. They are supposed to comfort. I know that. But I want to scream at everyone to shut up. What are *they* sorry for?

In the afternoon, my dad and Holden make several trips back and forth to the restaurant to bring the food over there. None of us want it. Instead, my mom and Sara make plain pasta, and we all try to force it down. My dad tells us what the plans are for tomorrow, but no one responds. I keep waiting for my mom to look up. To look at us. Look at me. But she doesn't. Maybe it's because she can't. Maybe it's because she knows it's my fault.

The next morning, Sara wakes us all up, and we take turns in the shower. I don't own any skirts, so Sara lends me one of her Indian print ones. It's too long, so I have to roll it up at the waist. I wear a dark blue blouse with it. Standing in front of the mirror, I don't recognize myself. My hair hangs limply to my shoulders. I look frumpy. Sara comes into my room with a brush and offers to pull my hair back for me. When she's done, she leads me to the mirror again. Somehow, with my hair up, I look taller. Older.

"You should pull your hair back more often, Fern. You look pretty."

I don't want to look pretty.

Sara looks older, too. She has on a long, deep purple skirt with a black ballet-style top. She wears a pretty shawl over her shoulders that Mona knitted for her for Christmas last year. When our eyes meet, she looks down, and for a second, she looks just like my mom last night. And I realize why they can't look at me. Because they think it's my fault. Because they know it is.

I follow Sara downstairs to join the others. My mom looks small. She's wearing another Mona shawl. She looks like she's hiding in it. My dad wears an old suit that looks too tight. They are both pale and distant looking. Holden hands me my coat and helps me put it on. I feel Charlie's fireman in my pocket and bite my bottom lip. I don't want to cry today. I just want to be a stone.

The parking lot is already filling up when we get to the restaurant. We park in the back and go in through the kitchen. It's been almost a week since I've been here. A few of the regular cooks are busy heating up the various dishes people dropped off. They hug my mom and dad and cry. We inch closer to the swinging door that leads to the dining room, where people are already gathering.

The door swings open and the minister comes in. He shakes my dad's hand and pats my mom's shoulders.

"The chairs are all set up, and people are starting to settle in," he says.

My parents latch on to each other as if they are holding each other up. Sara and Holden both reach for my hands.

"The table looks beautiful," the minister says. "The flowers are perfect. I understand you didn't bring the urn with you."

My mom shakes her head.

I hadn't thought about an urn. That there would be one. My grandparents died before I was born, and I've never been to a funeral before. But I guess they must put the ashes in something. I squeeze my eyes shut to try to erase the thought of Charlie in some sort of vase. All of Charlie in some tiny bottle. It feels so wrong. So impossible.

We wait a bit longer in the kitchen while the minister

goes out to the dining room to welcome people. Though I guess *welcome* isn't the best word. The smell of all the food heating up is making me feel sick to my stomach. The tag inside the collar of my shirt starts to scratch.

Finally, the minister comes back to get us. There's a row of empty seats saved for us in the front of the dining room, and we all sit down. I don't look out at the sea of people crammed into the restaurant. I look at my hands in my lap. After we're all seated, the minister goes to the front of the room and stands next to the table with the flowers and Charlie's photo in a large frame. Charlie's brown hair looks like it's glowing, with the beautiful fall light shining through. Sara took the photo when she and my mom brought Charlie apple picking a week or so before – before. Holden and I didn't want to go, and my dad was working. They came home with apple-cider doughnuts and two bags of apples. Charlie kept pulling apples out of the bag to show me and Holden which ones he'd picked. We told him he couldn't possibly know which ones were which, but he just scowled at us and said, "Do, too."

"These are the times when words fail us," the minister says, making eye contact around the room. "It isn't often that I'm asked to preside over a child's memorial service. And I admit, when I am, I take pause. I wonder, like many of you are probably wondering, how this could happen? We search inside ourselves. We may even question our faith. But always, I do find faith."

All will be well, I think. What a load of crap. What is there to have faith in? That bad things happen? That life isn't fair?

"When my own sister died, a friend shared a poem with me by Merrit Malloy. It's called 'Epitaph,' and I've kept it in my wallet for years because I find comfort in the words."

He clears his throat and begins to read. It starts with the line "When I die," so I stop listening. I don't want to hear that word. I don't want to feel its meaning.

My hand tingles with the memory of Charlie's sticky one in mine. I reach over and take Holden's hand to stop the feeling. It's warm and dry, and he holds on as tight as I do.

" 'Look for me in the people I've known,' " the minister reads.

I close my eyes. *No, Charlie. No. I want to see all of you, not pieces.* I squeeze Holden's hand harder and feel tears slip down my cheeks. My throat aches so much. I am choking on these words.

"'Love doesn't die, people do,'" the minister continues. "'So, when all that's left of me is love, give me away.'"

He says the last words very slowly, carefully, as if he wants to make sure their meaning sinks in. I hate them.

When all that's left of me is love, give me away.

How could I ever do that? Why would I want to do that?

"Today these words may seem too radical to bear," the minister says, as if he read my mind. "I know they were to me when I first read them. But over the years, as I think of my sister and the love she spread, I am inspired by this goal. Love doesn't die. No. Love never dies. And your love for Charlie will not fade. It will grow."

Beside me, I feel Sara's shoulders shake as she cries, and I reach over and take her hand in my free one.

"But do not let that love be out of guilt. You all provided Charlie with a beautiful childhood. Many of the people who work at this restaurant have shared stories about Charlie. About his beloved Doll and the pure joy he took in every moment. How he waited at the window every day for his sister Fern to come from school. How he loved his sisters and brother the way only a youngest child can."

I squeeze my sister's hand harder and on my other side, Holden's. I don't know if I can bear to hear more. I don't know if I can keep myself from screaming, I hurt so much.

"Charlie was a very special child. Like all children. And so I ask you today to embrace that love you have for Charlie. Let it heal your heart. Let it guide you tomorrow and all the days of your lives. That is the kind of love that is a gift you *can* give away and still never be without."

Warm tears drip down my cheeks, but I don't wipe them away. I clutch Holden's and Sara's hands tighter.

The minister bows his head, and we all do the same. There's a long, stretched-out silence that's only interrupted by the sniffs of people crying. And finally a quiet song the minister sings without any music. But I don't listen to the words, because all I can think of is Charlie and all that is left of him.

When the minister finishes singing, he quietly puts out the candle that was on the table.

And then it's over.

28

THE MINISTER MOTIONS for our family to stand, so we get up and walk to the back of the restaurant. Then people start to come toward us. There are so many. Regulars from the restaurant. People from school. Strangers. They hug my parents. And some of them hug me. I notice that not everyone is coming over to us and I'm glad. From the back, I see the staff bringing out food from the kitchen, and some people I recognize as regulars from the restaurant help spread the dishes out on a few tables they are already moving back into place.

"I'm so sorry for your loss. I'm so sorry." The familiar words thrum in my ears over and over again. Men's voices. Women's voices. Quietly. Gently. Someone hugs me and gets their wet tears on my cheek. I wipe them on my shoulder. I don't know why they make me feel sick.

Then Cassie is standing in front of me with her parents. She hugs me, but she doesn't say she's sorry. She doesn't say anything. She just holds on.

"You let us know if you need anything, honey," her mom says. "Anything at all. You come over any time you want." She and Cassie's dad both hug me, too. As Cassie walks away, she looks back at me over her shoulder, as if she's checking to make sure I didn't disappear.

When Gray comes up to us, he seems uncomfortable. "Hey, Fern," he says without looking at me. "I, um ... I'm really sorry about what happened. It sucks."

I nod.

He moves on to Holden, who doesn't say a word but wraps his arms around Gray and hides his face in his neck and cries into him. Gray looks like he doesn't know what to do. He also looks so *big* next to Holden like that. He's a lot taller and filled-out-looking next to skinny Holden. Gray holds him like he is more of a dad than a boyfriend. Like he wants to protect him. Their long hug starts to back up the line, so people start to go around them. At one point, I see my dad glance over with a sort of surprised look. It's the first time he's seen Gray, and I think maybe he is shocked to see just how much older Gray really is. Or maybe just to see them hugging.

I see Sara notice them, too. And I wish she had someone here to hold her like that. Or like Cassie held me. But all her friends are away at school. All she has is the restaurant staff to hang out with, and that can't be much fun since, except Gil, they're all way older than she is. For the first time, I realize how truly lonely she must be. I understand why she would sneak off to kiss Gil.

When Ran's parents get to me, they hug me close. I can feel all their unspoken words and sorrow in the way they hold me. I look around to see where Ran could be, but I don't see him anywhere, and they don't explain his absence.

When we finally get through the line of people and Holden lets go of Gray, the minister gathers my family into a small circle.

"You all holding up?" he asks.

No one replies, but I'm sure we're all thinking, *Not really.*

"Well, there is a beautiful spread here. Plenty of food and seats. If you need to get some fresh air, it will be fine to step outside. People will probably want to offer their support one more time before they leave."

My dad leads Sara and my mom to a table in the corner. My mom looks even more empty than she did earlier.

Holden and Gray walk over to another table, leaving me standing alone with the minister. He smiles at me and puts his hand on my shoulder. "Sara, I hope you and your family know that even though you don't belong to our church, you can call or e-mail me any time if you need someone to talk to. I know what an impossibly difficult time this is."

His face is so gentle and sincere, I can't bring myself to tell him I'm Fern.

"Thank you," I say.

He hands me a folded piece of paper. "This is for you to read from time to time. It's the poem I shared. I hope it will bring you comfort the way it does me." He squeezes my shoulder and turns to make his way to the people and the food.

I put the paper in my skirt pocket and walk toward the door.

Outside, the air is crisp and cool, despite the sunshine. I walk slowly through the parking lot to the picnic tables and sit down. I breathe in the cold air, letting it hurt my lungs. I cross my legs, careful not to kick Charlie – and then remember again for the thousandth time.

I feel the cold air against my ankles.

Charlie.

The carvings under my arm feel rough. I search for the names we carved – was it only last week? But there are so many, I can't find them at first. I run my finger over the area I'm sure we used and get a splinter. There.

Holden was here
Fern 2
& Charlie

I rub my aching finger on his name, knowing his fingers touched the same spot. I lean forward and put my cheek against the letters, trying to feel … I'm not sure what. The ache in my chest does its familiar move up my throat, but I swallow it back down. I swallow and swallow, my cheek pressed against the table, my finger bleeding over some other name.

With my head on the table, I hear car doors open and close as people begin to leave. And then the rustling of dried leaves behind me. Closer and closer.

I sit up and turn around.

It's Mr. Seymore. He's wearing a worn suit and clutching a light-blue envelope to his chest.

"I'm so sorry," he says, stepping closer. But when he says it, it's not like the others. When he says it, I know exactly what he means.

He holds out the envelope to me. It shakes in his wobbly hand.

"No," I say. I don't know what I mean. No, don't be sorry? Don't cry? Don't come nearer?

"Please," he says. He steps closer. "I didn't want to go inside. Didn't want to upset your folks. But I want your family to have this. I – I'm so sorry."

"It's not your fault," I say. I don't know what's in the envelope, but if it's money, it's something Mr. Seymore really shouldn't part with.

"It's my fault," I say. "I should have looked after him better."

He shakes his head. "I didn't see him. I didn't pull out that fast. Always take my time so I don't get into a fender bender. I've done that before. But I was being real careful."

"I know," I say. "You didn't hit him. You stopped in time."

"But I scared him, poor kid. And he fell back."

"He was running away from me. I was the Big Bad Wolf."

He shakes his head again. "Didn't see a thing. I looked. I was real careful."

"He was running," I say again. "He was running away from me. I wasn't playing with him, so he made up this game."

I wish he would stop shaking his head. It isn't going to make any of it not true.

He holds out the envelope again. "Please," he says. "It's not much, but—"

"I can't." I look again at his worn clothes and remember his old beat-up car. "It wasn't your fault. It was mine."

"Fern?" Ran walks toward us through the crunchy leaves.

Mr. Seymore turns toward him, then back to me.

"Please keep that," I say. "Please."

His mouth trembles, but he finally nods. He puts the envelope back inside his jacket. I see a hole in the worn elbow of his suit jacket when he bends his arm. He walks away slowly, careful not to trip on something hidden in the leaves.

When Ran reaches the table, he sits next to me so that our arms are touching. "I've been looking for you."

"I didn't see you earlier."

"I was having a hard time in there," he says.

I nod.

"You're bleeding."

"I know."

He reaches over and takes my hand. I didn't realize I'd put it back over the peace sign. Ran squints at it, then puts both our hands over the names again.

Ran's hand on mine is warm and strong. I lean my head on his shoulder and fill my chest with cold air again. I smell his familiar Ran smell. His shampoo and his laundry detergent and the outdoor smell of his jacket.

Ran is really the only one I feel like I could tell anything to, about how I'm feeling. But I stay quiet. Somehow, I think Ran already knows exactly how I feel. And exactly what I need.

Just quiet. Just a friend. And the impossible.

29

RAN'S PARENTS COME and get him at the table and hug me one more time before they all leave. The parking lot is mostly empty, and I know I should go back inside.

When I go in, I see that everyone is gone except for Gray and the restaurant employees. Most of the tables and chairs are back where they belong, and people are sitting in the middle where three tables have been pushed together the way we do on Thanksgiving and sometimes for special Sunday brunches. Since we don't really have any relatives, we always have family gatherings at the restaurant for the employees who don't have anywhere to go.

I sit at the nearest empty seat, between Mona and Trevor. A few people are eating, but mostly everyone plays with their food. Holden absentmindedly makes a mint-green Jell-O mold jiggle back and forth.

It seems like none of us really wants to be here, but no one wants to leave, either. Beyond the group, Charlie's photo and the flowers have been moved to his favourite booth. I wonder who did it.

"Fern," my dad says from the other end of the table, "would you mind going up to get your mom and Sara?"

"I can go," Gil says, starting to stand up.

"It's OK. I'll go," I say.

As I climb the familiar stairs, I let my hand dangle by my side and wait for Charlie's sticky fingers to grasp it. I walk more slowly, wishing, wishing, wishing for that familiar tug, even though I know it will never come.

When I get to the office, the door is partially closed. The first thing I notice is that my mom's sign has been torn off the door. I know this because there's a ripped piece of paper still under the thumbtack that held it up.

"I can't look at him," I hear Sara say on the other side of the door. "I can't face him." I can tell she's crying.

"Being with Gil has nothing to do with what happened," my mom says quietly.

"Yes, it does!" Sara says. "If I hadn't been with him, I would have been in the dining room. Mr. Seymore would have left sooner. Maybe Charlie wouldn't have even gone looking for Fern."

"And maybe if I hadn't been up here trying to escape – trying to – oh, God." She makes that strange noise she made the morning she found Charlie. Then she starts to sob.

"Mom, Mom, stop," Sara says.

I peek around the door and see them sitting on the floor. All of my mom's meditation stuff is strewn around the room. My mom is rocking back and forth, pulling at her hair with her hands.

"Please stop," Sara cries. "You have to stop. We need you."

My mom stops rocking and looks at Sara. "Oh, honey," she says, and opens her arms to her. Sara leans in, and my mom hugs her tight. She rubs her back in familiar circles, as if she's a little kid. As if she's Charlie.

I stand there quietly, thinking about their guilt. How all this time, they weren't blaming me; they were blaming themselves. And I want to blame them, too. I want to hate them. But I also want to be the one in my mom's arms. I want to be the one she says *It's not your fault* to.

I open the door just a little, and it creaks.

They look up at me through their watery eyes.

"Dad sent me to come get you," I say quietly.

My mom sees me eyeing her meditation stuff on the floor. Ripped pieces of her sign are scattered around the room like snow.

"What happened in here?" I ask.

My mom turns away and starts shaking her head.

I pick up the singing bowl Charlie used to love to play with and put it back on its shelf.

"Leave it," my mom says. "I don't want it anymore."

I wait for her to say something else to me. Something to make me feel like I'm still her daughter, too. Doesn't she know I need her? A normal mom would. She'd put my pain before hers. I want to hate her for it. But as I look at her, I realize she doesn't have control of her pain; it controls her. It's what's making her disappear.

"Will you come downstairs?" I finally ask. But really I want to say, *Will you hold me? Please, will you just hold me?* The familiar ache in my throat grows, and I feel like I'm going to choke.

"In a minute," she whispers. "We'll be down in a minute."

Sara looks up at me finally, and I see all the hurt that I feel in her eyes. But she doesn't get up. She just stays there on the floor with my mom and all the broken pieces.

So I leave them there. Because I don't know what else to do. And it hurts too much to stay.

Back at the table, I tell my dad they'll be down soon. I wonder what he'll think when he sees what my mom did to the office. I always hated it when she went off and shut herself away from us, but seeing her now, like she's lost her inner peace forever, only makes me feel scared. Like we've lost her, too.

"I really loved that kid," Patrick says, setting a casserole dish down in the middle of the table. "That was some special kid."

"There was something about Charlie," Mona agrees. "Remember that time when he took off all his clothes and ran around the dining room during the dinner rush?" She slaps the table and laughs so hard she starts to cough.

Dwayne reaches over and pats her on the back. "That kid was awesome," he says.

"Remember when he begged me to let him be assistant busboy, and he just started clearing away everyone's plates, even though they weren't done yet?" Trevor asks.

"Oh, yeah," says Mona. "He took away Mrs. Abbot's bowl of soup, and the old battle-ax chased him all the way to the kitchen!"

Everyone laughs. Even my dad smiles, though it looks like it hurts.

I don't want to hear these stories.

I dig my nails into my palms and concentrate on the heaps of unidentifiable food on the plate someone put in front of me, but it makes me feel sick, so I push it away.

"Oh, remember when he climbed out on the roof with his doll?" Gil asks. "It was during the lunch rush, and no one noticed he'd wandered off. Then Fern came charging into the dining room from outside. She said, 'Charlie's on the roof!' and bolted up the stairs. Remember that, Fern? You were, like, a hero!"

"Oh, yeah. That was awesome," Patrick says, nodding.

I remember that day. I was so mad that my mom had lost track of Charlie long enough that he'd climbed out on the roof without her even noticing. And it wasn't during a lunch rush. She was just bussing tables, casually chatting with Mona and Gil. I remember racing past them and up the stairs. I had already crawled out on the roof through the office window before my mom leaned out to ask what I was doing, then screamed when she saw Charlie. He was sitting on the edge of the roof, dangling his feet over the side. My heart was pounding so hard, I thought I was going to be the youngest kid on record to have a heart attack.

"Them cahs don't look like ants," he'd said to me thoughtfully as I crawled closer to him.

"What?"

"In my show. Fum on top a building, cahs look like ants."

I moved in behind him and hugged him to my chest. "No, Charlie. That's from the top of a skyscraper. Not a small building like this."

"Oh," he said sadly.

I slipped my hands under his arms and dragged him back through the window to safety. My mom, Mona, and Gil cheered and hugged us. My mom took Charlie from me and held him close, as if he was a prize she had just won. She wouldn't look me in the eye.

I grit my teeth as I listen to Gil chuckling about it.

A few people get up and refill their plates with food while others continue to share stories about Charlie. I can't tell, but it looks like Holden and Gray are holding hands under the table.

Everything feels so strange. So wrong. People keep laughing as they share Charlie stories. It's like everyone forgot that the kid they're talking about isn't here anymore. That he's never coming back. Every time someone laughs, I feel myself getting angrier.

"Oh, remember that time when he took all the pots out of the lower cabinets and made a house inside and refused to come out?" Trevor asks.

I remember that day. I had to crawl in and get him. I remember I yelled at him because I'd torn my favourite jeans on the cabinet when I crawled in after him. And everyone gave me dirty looks like I was the worst big sister ever.

They all laugh again.

"Stop it!" I yell. I wasn't expecting to, but it just comes out. Loud. I stand up. "Stop talking about him like he isn't dead!"

It's the first time I've said the word out loud, and it hangs in the air like a terrible, terrible cloud, sucking all the laughter out of the room in an instant.

"It's OK, Fern," my dad says. "People need to do this." But he looks as miserable as I feel.

"No, they don't!" I yell. "It isn't right!"

They look at me in shock. Offended. Like I'm some little brat spoiling their party. Like once again I'm the one being mean to Charlie.

"You shouldn't be laughing! You shouldn't be talking about him like ... Charlie is *gone*! He is *never* coming back! And you're all *laughing*!"

My dad gets up and starts coming toward me.

"Fern," Holden says. "Stop it."

"He's dead!" I yell, ignoring him. "Charlie is dead!"

My dad is pulling me backward. His hands squeeze my arms hard as he pulls me, and I welcome the pain. Anything to make the other pain I feel go away. But I know it can't. I struggle so he'll squeeze harder.

"Come on," he says calmly. "Let's go outside."

He drags me to the door. Holden gets up, too, but my dad motions for him to stay.

The restaurant is totally quiet except for me struggling in my dad's arms.

"He's dead!" I yell one more time before the door slides closed. "He's dead."

30

As soon as we get outside, my dad lets go of my arm. I run to the picnic table and crawl below. The underside is covered with more carvings and dried-up gum in different colours. I pull my knees to my chest and try to disappear.

My father's footsteps crunch in the leaves and stop next to the table.

"Fern," he says.

I pull myself into a smaller ball.

He sits down and leans under. "I don't think I can fit in there."

I shift my body a little so my back is to him.

"All right." He sighs and bends down, struggling through the space between the seat and the tabletop. He finally manages to squeeze himself under. He sits cross-legged, facing me. And waits.

"Fern," he says quietly. "Look at me."

I shake my head, keeping my face covered with my arms.

He touches my arm, then gently pulls his hand away.

"You seemed pretty angry in there."

"I'm not going to apologize," I say.

"I wasn't going to ask you to." He shifts and bumps his head. "Not very comfortable under here, is it?"

"Charlie liked it."

He nods.

"I know how upset you are," he says. "I understand."

"No, you don't," I say.

"Well, I want to. Will you talk to me?"

"Everyone was acting like Charlie was just some happy memory. Like they've already moved on. I don't want to move on! I don't want him to be just a memory. I want him back."

"We all do," my dad says quietly.

"And everyone knows it's my fault, but no one will admit it. Mom and Sara blame themselves a little, but I think they also blame me. They won't look at me. Mom won't even … She hasn't even … I want her to hold me. But she doesn't. She's like a stranger."

My dad reaches over and touches my knee. "This is impossibly hard on everyone," he says. "We're all trying to cope in our own way."

"But I need her! I need her to be my mom! Why can she hold Sara but not me?"

"I'll hold you," he says, and he leans forward and pulls me to him. He rubs my back the way my mom used to, but it doesn't feel the same.

"We're being punished," I say into his dress shirt. "We didn't pay enough attention to him, so he got taken away from us. We didn't deserve him."

"No."

"Yes!"

"No. You know that's not true. Life doesn't work that way."

"There has to be a reason!"

"Stop it, Fern. Just … stop. Could we have paid more attention to Charlie? Sure. Heck, I know there were times when it was my turn to watch him and I'd get distracted by other things. But, honey, God doesn't punish little kids for other people's mistakes. It doesn't work that way."

I want to believe him. But I know he's wrong. Kids suffer because of other people all the time.

"We have to stop blaming," he says. "All of us."

I wonder if that means him, too.

"You really don't think it's my fault?"

"No. I really don't."

"But—"

"It's hard enough that he's gone. Trying to blame someone, trying to find a reason why – it won't change anything." He gently takes hold of my arm. His hand feels warm and strong. "Look at me," he says.

I lift my eyes to his.

"I love you. I love our family. If we're going to survive, we've got to stick together. We have to love and support one another."

But what if they don't love me back? What if they can't?

"Do you understand? Do you see how important that is?" His eyes are pleading. And sad.

I nod.

"Thank you." He looks out across the parking lot

toward the restaurant. The delivery truck is parked out back, but you can still see it: Charlie's giant face smiling at us.

"I suppose we'll have to paint over that," he says. "Can't imagine covering up his face, though." A tear slips along his jaw.

I move closer to him and lean against him again. He puts his arms around me and holds tight. Thoughts of Charlie swirl between us. Images of Charlie under this table, trying to tie my shoelaces together as I do my homework. As I ignore him.

When my dad finally lets go, he looks around again at the table that was Charlie's hideout. "I don't know what Charlie loved so much about playing under here," he says. "It's really pretty gross."

"Charlie didn't notice that kind of stuff," I say. I picture his dirty face, his crazy hair. His sticky hands. I smile, and a tiny hint of warmth enters my chest. "He was kind of gross, too."

My dad looks up at the tabletop roof. "Now I know why his hair was sticky all the time."

I almost laugh but stop myself.

"It's OK, Fern. Charlie wouldn't want you to be so sad."

But I've already swallowed it down.

"Should we go back inside? It's pretty cold out here."

I shake my head. "It hurts too much. Hearing those stories."

"I know."

"I mean it hurts so much, I can hardly breathe."

He nods. "I know."

"I feel like … like…"

"I know," he says. "It's OK. We can stay right here."

I picture my mom and Sara upstairs in the office, surrounded by their own guilt. And Holden and Gray, sitting at the table listening to all those Charlie stories, looking miserable. But they all have each other. And I guess I have my dad. But what I really want is Charlie.

My dad shifts again and rubs his lower back.

"You can go back in, Dad. I'll be OK."

He smiles at me but looks uncertain.

"I promise," I say. But I think we both know it's a lie.

"All right," he says. "I'll just go back in for a bit, and then we'll all go home." He squeezes himself out from under the table, and I listen to his feet slowly crunch through the leaves as he walks away.

31

WHEN HOLDEN COMES TO GET ME and takes me to the car, everyone is already waiting. I climb in the back and stare out the window. Sara sits in the middle between Holden and me. No one says a word as we drive home. No one asks me to sing to him. No one asks me to make Doll dance. No one reaches for my hand to hold and squeeze. No one whispers, *I love you, Ferny.*

At home, I go straight to my room and shut the door. I crawl into bed with the answering machine and hold it to my chest. I don't play it, just hold it. Hold all that I have left.

Eventually I hear everyone come upstairs to get ready for bed. My dad knocks on my door and comes in to say good night. He holds me close and pats my hair as if I'm a little kid. As if I'm ... I close my eyes and concentrate on his big hand, gently patting me. Soothing me.

"Get some sleep," he says. "We'll talk more in the morning." No one else comes to say good night.

I wait for the house to get quiet before I use the bathroom and brush my teeth. On my way back to my room, I stop in Charlie's doorway. It's dark, but I can see that his bed still isn't made.

I step inside and take a slow, deep breath. The air smells stale but still like Charlie's room. Like unwashed hair and baby powder, which he loved to coat himself with after his bath.

I feel along the wall and turn on the light. I look at each wall, plastered with crayon drawings. Each piece of furniture. Each toy still on the floor. I pick up one of his books and put it back on his bookcase. When I do, I see a small brass vase on the top shelf. I step closer. I've never seen it before. I reach out for it but then pull my hand away.

It's not a vase. It's an urn.

It's Charlie. In that small metal … thing.

I think about the answering machine and how it feels like he's alive in there. Not like this cold metal object on the top of a bookshelf.

I sit on the floor and stare up at it.

"I miss you," I whisper.

The room is quiet.

I wait and wait for him to answer somehow. To feel something. But the room is still.

Under Charlie's bed, I see a bunch of stuffed animals, some stray plastic dinosaurs, and a few board books he outgrew. Most of them have chew marks at the corners. I used to hate reading those to him because they were usually either wet or sticky. I reach for one and pull it out. It's *Big Red Barn,* one of his favourites. I open it and look up at the urn again. Waiting to feel something.

I begin to whisper the familiar first sentence.

As I read, I remember Charlie next to me, finishing each line.

Cat, he'd whisper, pointing.

I pause as I read, waiting for his voice to fill the silence.

I imagine him leaning against my arm, reaching for my ear.

And when I finish, I wait for what always comes next.

Again.

I hold the book to my chest and breathe and breathe what I can of his room and its memories. Then I get up and make Charlie's bed. I set some of the stuffed animals on it. Just his favourites. I put the book on his pillow. When I turn to leave, I see my mom standing in the doorway.

I jump back and almost fall on the bed.

"I didn't mean to scare you," she says. "I – I saw the light on."

She stays in the doorway. She has her shawl on over her nightgown. She looks even less like my mom standing there in the shadows, all sunken in on herself. As if she really is slowly disappearing.

"I was just…" But I don't know what to say.

Her hands shake as she fiddles with a loose piece of yarn on her shawl. "I heard," she says. "He loved that book."

She puts one foot into the room, moving into the light, as if she is finally going to come over and comfort me. But she pauses, as if she isn't sure she can.

Because she blames me. I know she does.

"He just ran away from me," I say. "I tried to catch up, but he was too fast."

"I know," she says.

"But you can't even look at me. You blame me. I know you do."

"No, Fern."

"Yes, you do! You haven't even touched me since it happened. You can't!"

"No."

"You know it's true!"

"No. Oh, honey, No. Come here." She steps back into the dark hall, as if she doesn't want me to see her up close in the light. See just how much the pain has changed her. But I already have.

Slowly, I go to her, even though I'm afraid.

In the hallway, it's shadow-dark except for the Snoopy night-light.

"I want you to be my mom," I tell her quietly. "I just want you to love me again."

"Oh, Fern." She takes my hand and pulls me close. "I do love you. Always." She holds me against her chest and rocks me back and forth. It feels so strange at first. She doesn't smell like I remember. And my face doesn't reach the part of her body it used to when she would hold me like this. I know it's because I'm bigger now, but to me it feels like she is smaller.

"I'm so sorry, honey. I'm sorry."

There are so many words I want to say back. I want to let it all out, the way I used to when I was little and she would hug me tight and I would tell her whatever was wrong, and she would rub and rub and rub my back in slow, strong circles and say it would all be OK.

All will be well.

"I need you," I cry into her scratchy wool shawl. "I need you." I squeeze my arms around her more tightly, waiting.

"I know, honey," she says against the top of my head. "I know … I know," while her own tears wet my hair. And finally her arms squeeze me back. "I'm here. I'm here now. Hush, now. I'm here."

32

IN THE MORNING, my dad makes us chocolate-chip pancakes. They don't taste right, but I force them down. Then he reminds Holden and me that we have to go back to school. I think he's convinced that the sooner we all go back to our normal routine, the sooner we'll get back to normal ourselves. But he must know deep down this will never happen. We will never be normal again.

On the way to school, I sit in my usual place alone in the backseat and stare out the window. Holden sits up front with my dad. When we get to school, I feel like I'm going to throw up.

"OK, you two. I know you don't want to be here, but you can't stay out forever. Call me if it's too much and I'll come get you right away."

"It's too much," Holden says.

"It is," I agree.

My dad nods. But he doesn't offer to take us back home.

Holden sighs and gets out of the car. For the first time, he actually waits for me. Together, we walk toward the large entrance and step inside.

The first bell rings as we make our way down the busy hall. People look at us in the predictably *I feel so sorry for you* way, but no one says it out loud. When we get to my locker section, Holden stops. "You going to be OK?"

I shake my head. "You?"

"Probably not. I'll meet you after school at the usual place."

"OK."

He joins the sea of people moving down the hall.

Ran and Cassie are waiting for me at my locker. They don't ask if I'm OK. They don't try to hug me. They just quietly wait for me to get my things and lead me to homeroom.

I spend the day feeling like I'm a new kid at a new school. Like suddenly even the people I've known since kindergarten are strangers, and they are all looking at me with curious eyes. Like I am an outsider because of what's happened. At the start of each class, I tell myself as soon as it's over I'll call my dad to come get me, but then I survive that class and go on to the next one. And then the day is over.

After school, my dad is waiting for us at the curb. I get in the car and we wait for Holden, who comes out about a minute later, holding his phone to his ear.

He opens the front door but doesn't get in. "Hey, um, change of plans. I'm way behind, so Gray and I are going to the library."

"Well, I'll give you both a ride," my dad says.

"Gray's picking me up. He goes to the Academy, remember?"

"Oh," my dad says. "Right."

"I'll be home for dinner," Holden says. He walks away before my dad even replies.

"Come on up front," my dad says to me.

I do, and we slowly pull out of the crowded pickup zone.

Instead of going home, we go to the restaurant.

The dining room is empty except for one older couple sharing a banana split.

I sit at Charlie's favourite booth and get my homework out.

"Want me to make you a milk shake?" Sara asks, suddenly standing over me.

"No, thanks," I say.

But she doesn't walk away.

"I got Mom to come to work today," she says quietly. "She's upstairs."

I nod.

She sits across from me. "I talked to Dad," she says. "And I want you to know, I don't think what happened is your fault." She reaches across the table and squeezes my hand. "You have to know that. And I'm sorry if I made you feel that way."

I try to pull my hand away, but she squeezes harder.

"I just – I blamed myself, too. Just like Mom. If we'd been watching him so you could do your homework, it wouldn't have happened."

And for a minute, I want to say, *Yes, you're right. It was your fault, not mine. If you'd been doing your job, he would have been with you instead.*

But he was with me.

And it wasn't because they were neglecting him. Not really. He was with me because he wanted to be.

"I was the only one who could have stopped him," I say. Deep down, everyone knows that. "But I couldn't. He was so fast. He just took off and—"

"Don't you get it?" She squeezes my hand again. "There are a million things we all could have done to change what happened. But we didn't know. We couldn't. And we can't go back and do those things now. It just happened, Fern. Not because of Mom. Not because of me or Dad or anyone else. And not because of you."

I close my eyes because I don't want to cry.

Sara reaches for my other hand and holds mine tight inside hers. "No one blames you, Fern. I promise."

I raise my eyes so we're staring into each other's souls. I never thought she knew about the tell-me stare, but it feels the same.

"I believe you," I say.

She pulls our hands toward her and lays her head against them. "I love you," she whispers.

The bell on the door tinkles. She lifts her head, and we both look toward the door as Ran and Cassie walk in.

"We thought you might need help catching up," Cassie says when they get to our table.

Sara smiles and gets up so they can sit with me. "I'll be upstairs with Mom." She walks away before I can respond. Before I realize I didn't tell her I love her back.

Cassie sits across from me and scoots along the seat to make room for Ran. If Charlie was here, he'd squish himself right between them. He'd hand Doll to Cassie, and he'd snuggle his head against Ran and ask for a story. And Ran would tell him one because that's the kind of person Ran is. And I would feel jealous.

Instead, the three of us just sit quietly. They get out their homework and give me their notes. But when I open my notebook, my pen feels so heavy. And everything just seems too hard.

"I'm getting a sundae," Ran says. "What do you guys want on it?"

Cassie smiles. "Everything."

He comes back with three spoons and a giant bowl overflowing with so many toppings, you can't see any ice cream. I slide all my stuff into my backpack, and we start to eat. For the first time, I can taste. I taste the sugar and vanilla in the fresh whipped cream. The chocolate sauce and butterscotch. We eat spoonful after spoonful. It's so much easier to eat than to talk. When we finish, we all lean back. Ran finally takes off his zipped-up sweatshirt. He's wearing his BE T-shirt.

"Let's try again," he says. And this time they help me take notes, and we talk a little bit about school, and they remind me that the homecoming dance is coming up. It's a huge event for the middle school and high school because it's one big dance. Every year, a group of parents gets together to try to separate the two groups, but there's always another group that fights for the tradition, and they all end up agreeing to have more chaperones instead. Sara thinks pretty soon there will be more chaperones there than students.

As Cassie talks about the dance, she keeps glancing over at Ran with a hopeful look in her eyes, but he doesn't ask her if she wants to go.

When it's time to leave, Sara offers Cassie and Ran rides home, but they say they can walk. They each give me a hug and head off together. I wish I could go with them.

In the car, Sara drives, and my mom sits in the passenger seat. She leans her head against the window. I thought after last night, she would be more aware of the rest of us. Of me. But now I wonder if the hug in the hall will be my last one. I know it's selfish and awful of me, but I wonder if she would have been this sad if it had been me instead of Charlie. Charlie was her special joy. I know that. I never felt like the special youngest child before Charlie was born. Only that one day when I was sick. Most of the time I felt like the extra kid to clothe or take to the dentist. But when Charlie came along, my parents totally changed. They doted and coddled and adored. They filled a baby book with all of Charlie's firsts, while my own baby book remained mostly blank except for my birth date and how much I weighed. They called Charlie their autumn surprise. He was their gift. And I always wondered what that made the rest of us.

But I realize now, he was my gift, too.

I touch my ear.

I love you, Ferny.

Why didn't I know it? Why didn't I pay attention? I don't want to be the youngest again. I can't be.

At home, I go straight to my room and shut the door. I pull the answering machine from under my bed and plug it in. I press the side of my face against the speaker and wait for Charlie's happy, proud voice to vibrate against my cheek and imagine his sticky fingers are touching me. I play the message again. This time I put my hand on the speaker, as if mine is touching his. And listen again and again.

"Fern!" Sara calls from downstairs. "Dinner!"

I play the message one more time, trying to hold the words and his voice inside, even if they are a lie. Then I carefully put the machine back under my bed.

33

AT DINNER, my mom has a big glass of wine, and my dad has some sort of amber-coloured liquor in a glass. We're almost done by the time Holden shows up. When he comes in, his cheeks and lips are rosy red. He looks like he has a little of the glow he had the first time he came home from being with Gray. Until he sees my dad's expression.

"Where have you been?" my dad asks. He's on his fourth glass. He never drinks this much, and he seems different. At first, I was glad when he said he was going to come home to be with us for dinner from now on.

But now I'm not so sure.

"At the library," Holden tells him. "Remember? I told you I'd be there."

"You said you'd be home for dinner. We were worried."

Holden looks at the time on his cell phone. "It's only seven thirty. Sorry I'm a little late." He sits down and reaches for a serving dish of rice.

"Oh, no, you don't," my dad says.

"What?"

"You come late, you pay the price. No dinner."

"Are you kidding?"

I look at Sara, who is staring at our dad like he's a stranger.

"Go to your room," he says.

"What am I, ten?"

My dad slams his fist on the table. "Don't you talk to me in that tone! I said go!" Now he's scaring me.

Holden looks around at each of us as if to say, *Has Dad gone crazy?*

My mom reaches out for my dad's arm like that will help calm him down, but he brushes her off.

"Come on, Dad. Let him have some dinner," Sara says.

"Don't!" my dad yells. "Don't tell me what to do! You shouldn't be hanging around with that … that boy. He's too old. It's not right."

"Oh, give me a break. You don't care how old he is. Why don't you say what you're really afraid of, Dad?"

"Stop it! You don't know what you're talking about."

"You're afraid he's my boyfriend. You're afraid that I'm gay. Well, guess what? You're right! Is everyone happy now? I'm gay and Gray is my boyfriend, and you're just going to have to deal with it!"

My dad stands up and stumbles, knocking his chair over. "No. I do not have to deal with it! That boy is too old for you! He's probably eighteen or nineteen, for God's sake. You are fourteen years old, Holden!"

"George, please calm down," my mom says quietly. "Holden, we support you."

"We most certainly do *not*!" my dad yells. "It would be one thing if you were seeing someone your age. But this is unacceptable!"

"I support you," I say. "Gray is nice. Who cares if he's older?"

"Me, too," says Sara. "Gray's OK, Dad. Don't worry."

"I don't care if he's OK. He is too old for Holden, and that's final."

"What do you mean 'that's final'?"

"You're not to see him again."

"Are you kidding me?"

"George, let's talk about this later," my mom says quietly. "You've obviously had too much to drink."

"Forget it. I'm outta here," Holden says. "This family is insane."

"Oh, no, you don't!" My dad starts to walk toward Holden, but he's already out of reach. The door slams as Holden takes off once again.

My dad just stands there, as if he doesn't even know how he ended up where he is.

This is the time in the conversation when Charlie should be piping up with some random comment to break the tension. It's quiet, as if we're still waiting for him. It's strangling us.

"I give up," my dad finally says. "I just give up." He storms upstairs.

My mom drinks the rest of her wine and goes after him.

"That went well," Sara says sarcastically.

"I've never seen Dad like that," I say.

"He'll come around. He's just drunk. I think he was really worried when Holden was late – that's all. He just freaked out. It's normal to worry more after everything that's happened. He'll be fine once he gets used to the idea of Holden and Gray."

"You really think so?"

She shrugs. "Yeah. I do. He's just crazy right now. I mean, he's always a little crazy, but—"

"But not mean. Not like tonight."

"Don't worry, Fern. Mom'll talk to him."

"What about Holden?"

"Holden knows how to take care of himself. He always has. And thank God his secret is finally officially out of the bag. At least now we can all stop pretending."

She gets up and starts clearing the table, so I do, too.

"Dad'll come around, Fern," she says. "I know he will."

Right. And Mom will get back to normal. And everything is going to be fine. All will be well. Maybe we can stop pretending about Holden. But what about everyone else?

34

ALL THAT WEEK, Holden and my dad avoid each other. After school, Gray picks up Holden, me, and now Cassie and Ran, and we go to the restaurant to do our homework. Mona brings us snacks, and we make our own sundaes. Then they leave. Somehow, this gets me through the week. But every day away from *that* day makes me feel more lost and away from Charlie. So the first thing I do when I get home is go to my room, shut the door, and listen to his voice.

The following Monday, Sara's back on car duty. On our way to school, Holden turns around toward me and grins. "So, Fern, did Ran ask you to Homecoming yet?"

I feel myself blush. "No. We're just friends. Plus I'm not going."

"Why not?"

"I don't feel like having fun."

"Oh, come on, Fern. It would be good for you," Sara says.

"It totally would," Holden says. "And Ran is so cute."

"We're just friends."

"Then go as friends!" Holden says.

I picture me and Ran at the dance. Me in a dress, him in a shirt and tie. We look strange. Ran and I belong in T-shirts and jeans.

"Isn't anyone going to ask who I'm going with?" Holden asks. He's smiling like a goofball. He looks like he did that night he came home just before my dad went psycho.

"Seriously?" Sara asks.

"Yup. I told Gray about it last night, and he said yes."

"Wow," I say.

"We're going shopping for tuxes after school. Want to come with us, Fern?"

"You'd want *me* there?"

"Yeah! It'll be great! Gray will take us after school. We could totally use a girl's opinion."

I eye him carefully. Does he really want to go there with Gray? As a couple? What if the Things see them? Well, I guess if they're at Homecoming, they'll see them anyway. *You're brave,* I think. *You're really brave.* But out loud I just say, "OK."

Sara clears her throat, and Holden stops smiling. "What?"

"Are you going to tell Dad?"

Holden sighs. "Eventually. Let me enjoy a few stress-free days, all right? Jeez."

"Hey, I'm happy for you! I just want you to be realistic about this. You do remember Dad's little freak-out, right?"

"He'll come around."

"I know, but this might be a bit too much too soon for him."

"Too bad. This is how it is." Holden turns away and stares out the window.

"Hey, I didn't mean to bum you out. You're right. It'll be fine."

But she doesn't sound very convincing.

I lean back in my seat and feel the emptiness beside me. For five minutes, it felt like we were our regular family again. I put my hand on the seat where Charlie should be and close my eyes. I try to feel something. I'm not sure what. Just … *Charlie*. I think about the poem the minister read at the funeral. *When all that's left of me is love, give me away.* And I wonder how he could believe that makes any sense. All I want to do is hold on. I press my hand down on the seat and try again to feel some trace of him. Some light tingle that says, *I'm here.* But before I know it, the car stops and we're at the drop-off lane and it's time to get out.

After school, I meet Holden and Gray out front, and we head to Manny's Tails. The store is crowded with circular racks of black and gray fabric. Holden is practically bouncing, he's so excited. Gray is calm and cool, as usual. Maybe even more than usual.

Before we can start exploring, a tiny man in a dark suit comes up to us. "Hello, folks." He eyes each of us up and down. "How can I help you today?"

"We want to rent two tuxes," Holden says.

Suit man claps his hands together. "Is this for the homecoming dance at the high school?"

"Yeah," Gray says unexcitedly.

Suit man steps back and looks both Holden and Gray up and down again, squinting one eye.

"I bet you're a thirty-six regular," he says, sizing up Holden. "And you're about a forty-two. I'll be right back. I'm Manny, by the way!" he calls from behind a rack.

Holden gushes at Gray. "Should we get matching?" he asks.

"No way," Gray says coolly. "That's so gay."

Holden laughs and elbows him.

"OK, here we are, guys," the salesman says. "And which of these studs is your man, honey?" he asks me.

I snort and Holden laughs again. Gray smirks. "I'm his sister," I say, pointing at Holden.

"She's our fashion consultant," Holden adds.

"I see." Manny holds out a jacket for each of them. "You boys get sent on a mission from your girls? That's nice they trust you. Most girls come with their boyfriends and make all the decisions."

Holden and Gray don't say anything. Gray seems to shrug off the comment as no big deal, but Holden looks like he's trying to decide if he should tell Manny the truth. They button up their jackets, and Manny steps back to inspect them. "Yes," he says, nodding at Gray.

"No," he says, shaking his finger at Holden. "I'll be right back."

Gray walks over to the mirror to check his jacket. "It looks great," Holden says. "Let me try it."

"It would be way too big for you," Gray says. He turns this way and that, checking himself out. I'm starting to wonder what Holden likes about him. He's nice enough, but beyond the cool car and expensive clothes, what else is there?

"Here ya go, bud," Manny says to Holden when he comes back. Holden trades jackets with him. The new one definitely looks better.

"Let me get you guys some dress shirts to put on under those so you can get the full effect. Then I'll measure you for pants."

Holden and Gray disappear into the changing rooms with their shirts. In the far corner of the shop, I see a single rack of gowns of every colour imaginable. I go over and start sliding them across the rack, checking each one. The silky material feels so fine and fancy. I try to imagine myself in one of these, holding someone's hand.

"Sorry, hon. Those aren't for sale. We just use them for the mannequins."

"Oh." I blush and quickly pull my hand away from the fabric.

Back by the big mirror, Holden and Gray strut around in their tuxes.

"Coupla studs, huh?" Manny says, elbowing me.

"Yeah," I say.

Holden winks at me. But so far, that's about the first time he's even noticed me since we got here. I don't know why he wanted me to come so much if he was just going to ignore me.

When they decide on their styles, Manny asks them what colour their dates' dresses are, and if they want matching cummerbunds and ties. Again Holden looks at Gray. Maybe he's waiting for Gray to tell the guy the truth. But Gray just clears his throat and says, "We want black ties. No cummerbunds."

"Classy," Manny says.

Holden frowns and fiddles with the collar on his shirt. I wonder if he's thinking what I am: *Phony.*

"Let me write all this up for you while you change, and then you can give me your deposits," Manny tells them.

"I'll be outside," I say. I leave them in the store and stand out on the sidewalk. The street is busy and smells like car fumes and Dumpster. I look inside the shop window at the mannequins on display. The man mannequin holds the lady mannequin's hand. The lady wears a pink prom dress. They smile in their permanent way, as if they will never have anything happen to them to wipe the happiness away. It's sort of how Charlie looked. Always happy. Never worried. Even when he was grouchy, he still had that happy way about him. Just like Charlie in *Charlie and the Chocolate Factory*. Life was a wonder.

I reach forward and put my hand on the glass window and remember the scene in the book when Charlie gets to ride in the great glass elevator, rising up above everything and everyone, like a shooting star going in the wrong direction. Tears begin to drip down the side of my face faster than I can wipe them away. I realize I haven't cried yet today. And I'm not sure if I cried yesterday. And now I can't stop.

When Holden and Gray come out of the store, Holden is beaming. Gray is Mr. Cool. I let my hair fall across my face so they can't see I'm crying. But I don't need to worry because neither of them even looks at me.

We get in the car, and Gray cranks the radio. I don't ask where we're going next. Five minutes later, they pull up to Harry's and I climb out.

"Tell Mom I'll be home in time for dinner!" Holden says happily. As soon as I climb out, the car takes off.

It's sunny and a bit warm. I walk to the picnic tables and sit down. I find our names and trace Charlie's again with my finger. Over by the loading area, I can see the delivery truck. My dad asked Dwayne, Trevor, and Gil to paint over Charlie, but the paint they used was the wrong kind, and Charlie's face is starting to show through. His messy smile.

Whenever my parents' friends met Charlie for the first time, they would study his face, then look at each of us. "He looks just like his mother," they'd say. Or, "Looks like Holden at that age." People were always looking for traces of us in Charlie. But now I wonder if it will be the other way around. Will they stare at us, searching for traces of him?

When I go inside, Ran and Cassie are sitting at Charlie's table sharing a sundae. "Finally!" Cassie says. "Where've you been?"

I walk over to them and sit next to Cassie.

"What are you guys doing here?" I ask.

"It's our new thing," Ran says. "Remember?"

I just say, "Oh."

"And we also have an important announcement to

make," Cassie says. She looks too happy. Did she finally get Ran to go out with her? Why is my heart starting to ache?

"You do?" I say quietly.

"Yup! We're all going to Homecoming together. You, me, and Ran."

"As friends," Ran adds. "We think it will be good for you."

"It's all decided," Cassie adds. "And I even have something for you to wear. So you can't say no because you don't have a single excuse."

"Wow," I say. "You thought of everything."

"We really did!" Cassie says.

I think she is going to explode with excitement. "This is going to be great!" Holden says later that night when I tell him the news. He's standing in front of the bathroom mirror with a palm of hair gel. There's a magazine cutout of a guy's head taped to the bathroom mirror. His hair is shaggy, but in a perfectly sculpted sort of way.

"I'm going to wear my hair like this for the dance. What do you think?"

I inspect his head from all sides. "Kind of shiny," I say.

"The gel will dry."

"I guess I like it, then," I say. "It looks … different."

"Boy, Fern, way to lay on the charm. What'll you do with your hair? I think you should wear it up."

I shrug. I'm starting to dread the whole thing. Cassie and Ran will look beautiful. I know this. Because they just naturally are. And then there I will be looking frumpy in some hand-me-down dress with my mousy hair, and it will be obvious that the only reason I am there is because they feel sorry for me.

"So how are you getting to the dance?" Holden asks. "Because I think Gray and I will want to go alone in his car. Nothing personal but…"

"Cassie's parents will take us," I say. "And Sara will pick us up after."

He nods and turns his head this way and that, making sure he looks great from every angle. He doesn't even seem to notice when I leave him there and go to my room. I'm not his Phoebe anymore. Maybe I never really was.

I shut my door and pull out the answering machine from under my bed. I plug it in, sit on the floor, and hold it to my ear as Charlie quietly comes alive to promise me a lie.

35

ALL THAT WEEK, school buzzes with Homecoming preparations. There's a pep rally and a million announcements about how the dance will be alcohol free and that the dress code will be strictly enforced. And that because this is a schoolwide event, the high schoolers are expected to be the perfect role models for the middle schoolers. And there will be plenty of chaperones to make sure they are.

Every time I see Cassie in the hall, she gushes about some detail of our plans that she forgot. Ran just smiles quietly.

On Friday afternoon, the three of us are standing at our lockers before our final study hall. Cassie tells me how we all have to go to her house after school so I can try on my dress. I don't explain that it seems very late to be trying on my dress. What if it doesn't fit?

"We're the same size, and it fits me perfectly," she says.

I don't point out that we are not the same size. Cassie has these two things coming out of her chest – way out – that I do not yet have. I look there automatically and then quickly turn away, but my eyes catch Ran's and we both blush like crazy.

Luckily, the bell rings and I rush away from both of them to study hall before Cassie can make me promise I'll go. I sit in the crowded room with my elbows on my desk, my hands over my ears, trying to shut out the sound of happy chatter about the stupid dance. I watch Mrs. Dribble – who doesn't even seem to mind the noise for the first time in history – sip her secret potion, until our eyes meet and she gives me this horrible look of sympathy, like she knows how I must feel right now. Like she is so sorry for me. So I close my eyes and try to shut her out, too.

* * *

At Cassie's house, Cassie tells me to go into the upstairs bathroom and that everything I need will be hanging on the shower-curtain rod. I walk down the hall and pause in the doorway, almost afraid to look. But hanging over the bathtub is not the frumpy, hot-pink bridesmaid-style dress that I imagined, but a simple silver dress. It has pretty little sleeves, and the skirt part is covered with a second layer of something sheer, so that when the dress moves, the fabric looks alive.

I shut the door and quickly undress and slip the gown over my head. When I turn to look at myself in the full-length mirror behind the door, I have to peer closer at my face to make sure it's really me.

The dark circles under my eyes match the gray fabric. But when I fake-smile, they disappear a little, and I can see the old me there. I turn, letting the skirt swish around my legs. When I look down, I see a pair of pretty silver ballet slippers next to the tub. I put them on and stare at myself.

Cassie knocks on the door. "Don't forget the hair clip on the counter!" she yells through the crack.

There's a big silver bow on the counter that I assume goes with the dress, too. I pull my hair back and clip the bow in place.

Then I look again.

My neck looks longer than I knew it was.

I look so ... different. Older.

I step closer again and stare at my stranger self in the mirror.

You look so sad, she says to me with her eyes.

"I am," I whisper.

She nods. *I know.*

The familiar pain in my throat rises up, and I cover my mouth to hold in the sob that wants to escape.

I don't know who I am anymore.

I take off the dress and carefully hang it back up. Cassie's door is closed. I can hear her and Ran talking inside. Well, I can hear Cassie talking inside. She's saying something about next year and a limo.

I knock.

Cassie shrieks. "Ooh! Come in, come in!"

I open the door and find Ran and Cassie sitting on the edge of Cassie's bed with their eyes squeezed shut.

"OK, on the count of three, we're opening our eyes. One. Two. Three!"

They both look.

"Just me," I say.

"What happened? Didn't it fit? I was sure it would fit!"

"It fit."

"But we wanted to *see*!"

"Sorry." I look at my feet.

"Well, I should go home," Ran says. He avoids eye contact with me.

Cassie sighs dramatically. "Oh, Fern. You can be happy sometimes, you know. You don't have to be sad every second."

I see my face in the mirror again.

"I know," I say. "But … it's hard."

She stands up and hugs me. "I'm sorry. I'm not trying to push you. We're just worried about you – that's all."

"We know you'll be OK," Ran adds. "And it's OK to be sad. Or to feel whatever you're feeling. Everything is OK."

All will be well, I think. *Say it.*

Except it won't be. Because Charlie isn't coming back.

"Want me to take you home?" Ran asks.

"Sure."

Cassie follows us to the door. I hold the dress up

high in one hand so it won't touch the floor. "It's really beautiful," I say. "Thanks."

"I can't wait to see you in it! I just know you'll be gorgeous."

I smile and she squeezes my free hand.

Outside, Ran gets his bike. It's the kind with the pegs on the wheels for tricks. Once he's on, I step up on the back pegs. I wrap one arm around his waist and hold the dress up behind me with the other. We slowly make our way down the sidewalk, my silver dress billowing behind us like a too-light shadow trying to dance out of my arms.

36

IT'S SATURDAY. The big day. So far, Holden and my dad have been pretty good at avoiding each other. My dad gave up on coming home for dinner the past few nights because he's been busy at work, gearing up for the "big move," which means that Harry's Ice Cream is making its way to local convenience stores. My dad pulled the Harry's ad off of TV and went with an image of the front of the restaurant for the label instead.

But time is not on Holden's side because when my dad decides to come home for a break between the lunch and dinner rush, Gray also decides to show up with Holden's tux. And that's when, as Sara would say, the you-know-what hits the fan.

Holden runs for the door before my dad can get there. He grabs the tux from Gray and starts to shut the door, but my dad gets there before Gray can escape.

"What are you doing here?" my dad asks, glancing at Holden's tux.

"Uh, bringing Holden's tux to him. It's the dance tonight," Gray says, cool as can be. "Pick you up at seven, right?" he asks Holden.

Holden blushes. "I'll be ready."

"Hi, Gray," I say, peeking around my dad's shoulder.

"Hey, Fern."

My dad is not distracted. "Young man, how old are you?"

Gray straightens. He's taller than my dad. My dad straightens, too. But it just makes his enormous belly stick out farther.

"Seventeen."

"Do you know how old my son is?"

"Uh, fifteen?"

My dad shakes his head. I can tell Holden is pleading with every molecule in his body for my dad to just go with it. But there is no chance on earth that is going to happen.

"He is fourteen years old. *Fourteen.* Don't you think you are a little old to be dating my son?"

"Um, I'm just gonna go now."

"That's right. And please don't come back."

Holden tries to push past my dad, who is blocking the doorway. "Gray, don't listen to him. Come back at seven!"

"I don't know, man," he says, backing up. "Your dad is intense."

"I'll be there! Meet me there, OK! I'll call you!"

But Gray is already hurrying down the driveway.

"You are *not* going to the dance with that boy," my dad says. His face is bright red. "You aren't going. Period."

"How can you do this to me? It's not fair!"

"I'm doing it to protect you, Holden. Can't you see that?"

"Protect me from what? From having fun? Or are we never allowed to do that again?"

"I want you to have fun. With kids your own age."

I wish my mom were here to help talk some sense into my dad, but Mona took her away for a "girls' day off," whatever that means. When they left, my mom actually smiled at us when she said good-bye. And then she gave us each a hug. "You're getting so big," she whispered in my ear. "I love you, honey."

"I love you, too," I whispered. And then I almost asked her to stay. Because I realized she wouldn't see me in my dress. And she should. She's my mom. But instead, she's leaving me again. Why does she need a "girls' day off"? What did she need to meditate for? To escape. From us. From me. Before I could get really upset, though, I realized that she doesn't even know I'm going to the dance. My dad doesn't, either. I'm not sure why I didn't tell them. Maybe because I still might change my mind.

"Dad," I say. "Gray isn't a bad person. You don't need to worry."

"Stay out of this, Fern. You're too young to understand. I'm giving you my final word on this, Holden. You are not to go."

"You can't stop me, Dad."

"Oh, no?"

"No."

They stand facing each other. Holden is a lot shorter than my dad and only about one-third the width.

"How do you think you're going to get there?" my dad asks, towering over him as if he can just physically block him from leaving the house.

"I'll take him," Sara says, stepping into the room.

"With what car?" my dad asks. "Last time I checked, that car was registered in my name."

"Don't be insane, Dad. You're totally overreacting. So Gray's a little bit older. Or are you really worried because he's gay?"

"Don't say that."

Holden slumps into the big chair, the plastic around his tux crinkles as he lays it across his lap like a blanket. "I knew it."

"No, you did not! That is not what this is about!"

"What is it, then? You're seriously concerned about Gray's age?" Holden asks.

"Seventeen-year-olds like to party! And they like to … you know. They have certain expectations. You're not ready for that."

Holden stands up again. "God, Dad. Are you kidding? I'm not going to—"

"Just stop! You aren't going!"

"Fine!" Holden storms upstairs.

"I'm going back to work," my dad says, leaving me

and Sara in the living room. I watch him stomp outside. Instead of getting into the delivery truck, he takes the station wagon – the car that is supposed to bring me, Ran, and Cassie home from the dance.

I collapse on the chair. I'm sure Ran's parents can bring us home instead, but I'm still upset. It probably never even occurred to my dad that I might be going to the dance, too.

Sara crosses her arms and gets that look she has when she's cooking up a scheme. From upstairs, there's a lot of door slamming and loud music.

"It's not fair," I say quietly.

"I know."

We sit there for a while, the bass of Holden's music pumping through our veins.

"We have to do something," I say.

Sara's expression changes into a smile. "Yeah. We totally do. Plus hello? How are you going to get home now?"

"I'm sure Ran's parents can pick us up. Or maybe I just won't go. It's not that important."

"Yes, it is, Fern. It's important for both of you." She thinks for a minute, then smiles. "Feel like playing fairy godmother?" she asks.

"What do you mean?"

"Holden needs us to turn a pumpkin into a coach." I follow her to the window, and we look out at the driveway at the huge ice-cream truck. "And that's our pumpkin," she says, grinning at me.

It feels so good to have her look at me like that. "Seriously?" I ask.

"There's a spare set of keys on the hook in the kitchen," she says. We both race to the kitchen just to make sure. She pulls the keys off the hook and shakes them so they make a jingle sound.

"CinderHolden," I say.

And we both crack up.

37

AFTER I CALL CASSIE AND RAN to tell them I'll meet them at the dance, Sara and I go upstairs and pound on Holden's bedroom door. When he finally turns off the music and swings the door open to say, *"What?"* we both stop smiling. His face is splotchy from crying.

We're quiet for a minute. Than Sara clears her throat.

"Cinderella," she says in a high-pitched fairy-godmother voice. "You shall go to the ball."

"Ha-ha."

"We're serious," I say. "You're going! Call Gray and tell him to meet us there."

"How? Dad took the car."

"Yeah," I say. "But he didn't take the truck."

Sara dangles the spare keys in his face.

"No. Way." He reaches for the keys, but she holds them just out of reach.

"Get ready!" I tell him. "We have to leave at seven!"

He kisses me on the cheek and grabs his tux off the back of his closet door. "Some privacy, please?" he asks.

I race to my own room, shut the door, and turn to face my dress. I take a deep breath. Can I really? Should I? I reach forward and touch the soft fabric. I picture it flowing behind me and Ran as we pedaled home. I see Cassie's excited face when she invited me and think about all the trouble she went to so I could have the perfect dress. And I know the answer.

When I'm ready, I stand in front of the mirror and stare at the stranger in front of me. I move just a little, and the fabric dances around my legs.

"Hey-eh!" Sara says, coming in without knocking. "Where'd you get that dress? It's beautiful!"

I turn. "Cassie loaned it to me. It was her sister Maddy's."

"Oh, yeah, I think I remember that. She wore it to Prom. Don't tell, but you look way better in it."

"Thanks."

"Except, um ... You really need to do something with your hair."

I check it in the mirror.

"Here, let's put it up again." She grabs a brush and band from my dresser and pulls it back, then twists it up and somehow gets the band around it just right.

"There's a bow," I say. "On my dresser."

Sara holds it up and makes a face as if it's contaminated. "Um, no. Hold on. I have an idea."

She runs down the hall to her room and comes back with an armload of makeup. But first she shows me what she's holding in her hand. Three silver butterfly clips. They are tiny, with pretty sparkly wings.

"Where did you get those?" I ask. I've never seen her wear them.

She shrugs. "One time Mom and I saw them in a thrift store and I liked them, but I never really had a chance to wear them." She carefully attaches them to my hair in the back, then gives me a hand mirror and shows me how to hold it so I can see the back of my head in my closet mirror.

"Beautiful," she says.

"They are," I say, turning my head so that the

butterflies glitter in the light.

"And so are you," Sara says quietly. "Now, come sit on the bed so I can do something about that sad face."

I sit while she rubs colour into my cheeks, gently brushes silver sparkles on my eyelids to match the butterflies, and curls my lashes. When she's done, she walks me to the mirror again.

"Well, there you go," she says. "A real home-coming princess."

I turn and hug her. I squeeze my eyes shut to keep from crying. "Thank you," I say.

"Don't mention it." She looks like she's about to cry, too.

"I wish you could be at the dance with us," I say.

She smiles but in a sad sort of way.

"With Gil," I say.

She shakes her head. "No, we're through."

"How come?"

She looks away. "It's just too hard," she says. "Knowing how often I chose sneaking off with him in-stead of taking care of Charlie."

"It's not your fault, Sara. You know that."

"I know. But even so, I just can't. It wasn't meant to be, anyway. I mean, Gil's not really my type." But she says it more like she's trying to convince herself.

She turns me around so we're both looking in the mirror again. "I wish Mom and Dad were here to see you like this."

I shrug, like it's no big deal. But inside, I wish it, too.

"Come on, let's get Holden and blow this joint."

I follow her down the hall. When we pass Charlie's room, I feel a tug and pause. Sara stops and puts her hand on my shoulder. "It's OK to have fun tonight," she says. "He would want that."

I nod, and we keep walking. And I can't help it. I'm smiling.

38

SARA POUNDS ON Holden's door. "Your carriage awaits!"

We follow her outside, and she opens the passenger door of the truck for us. Before we get in, we pause to look at Charlie's enormous face under the bad paint job. "He would've loved this," I say.

"Come on." Sara walks around to the other side, and we all climb in. The truck jerks a bit while Sara gets used to the clutch, but pretty soon we're rolling down the driveway and on our way.

Sara fiddles with the radio and comes to a Rolling

Stones song. She cranks the volume, and Holden starts singing, "You Can't Always Get What You Want" at the top of his lungs. He elbows me, so I join him, even though I can't really sing. Sara joins in, too. I can't remember a moment like this, when we all seemed happy at the same time. Maybe when we were younger and going on a fun road trip with our parents. Maybe.

When we get to the school, I feel butterflies in my stomach and realize I never ate dinner. But it's OK because they're nervous butterflies, not hungry ones. Holden slides out and takes my hand, helping me so I don't trip on my dress. We stand by the open door.

"Hey," Holden says. "Thanks."

"No problem!" Sara says. "So, um, I guess I'll just hang out till the dance is over? Pick you up here at ten?"

"Uh, I think I'll be going out with Gray after."

"You sure that's a good idea? Dad's already going to lose it when he realizes where you are."

"If he's already mad, how much worse could it be? I figure I'll be grounded the rest of my life anyway, so I might as well live it up while I still can."

"Good logic. What about you, Princess Fern?"

I bite my lip. "Ten sounds good. I hope Ran and Cassie don't mind the truck."

"Of course they won't. I'll be here. Have fun, my princesses!"

We close the door and face the school. The gym doors are propped open, and music flows from inside.

"You can go first," I say. "So it doesn't look like you're taking your sister to the dance."

Holden smirks. "Fern, I'm probably going to be the only guy dancing with another guy. I hardly think you're going to hurt my reputation." He holds out his elbow, and I slip my hand through his arm.

"Come on," he says. "Let's go raise some eyebrows."

I laugh. That's what my dad used to say whenever he wanted us to do something wacky for the restaurant. "OK," I say. "Let's."

In the lobby, there are giant pumpkins on either side of the door and about a million parents lining the entrance to the gym, on the lookout for any mischief. I let my hand slip out from Holden's arm before anyone can really see us. The gym is already packed with people dancing under orange streamers. As I step inside, Cassie comes running toward me.

"OK, well, this is it," Holden says. "Don't do anything I wouldn't do!" He disappears into the crowd.

Cassie wraps her arms around me.

"You look beautiful! Wow!"

We step back and take each other in. Cassie is all in gold. Her dark curly hair and bronze skin look like they have flecks of gold, too. She looks stunning. "You, too!" I say.

"Come on, Ran's waiting," she gushes.

She takes my hand and leads me inside the orange wonderland. There are pumpkins everywhere and bales of hay instead of chairs to sit on. "Don't sit down," Cassie says. "The hay will stick to your dress. I've seen at least four girls picking hay off each other. They look like monkeys grooming!"

Lit pumpkins with stars carved in them light the refreshment tables. We find Ran standing in a corner by himself, happily sipping punch. He's wearing an old-fashioned-looking tuxedo with a silver shirt underneath. It has ruffles. But the funny thing is, on Ran it looks great. He owns that outfit. Standing next to him, I feel myself stand up straighter, prouder.

"You two match," Cassie says. And even though she's smiling, I hear the hurt in her voice.

Ran smiles shyly at me. "I thought we could, you know, be coordinated."

"Well, we're all silver and gold," Cassie says, already recovering. "Like the song in *Rudolph*?"

"Yeah," I say. And then for some reason, I just start laughing. Because I love that she can turn her sadness around so quickly. Ran puts his hand on her shoulder and laughs, too. And it feels so good. So good and new. And OK. It feels OK to be here with my two best friends, happy.

We dance to the fast songs and take turns dancing with Ran to the slow ones. A few times, we dance near Holden and Gray, who are hanging out with a group of upperclassmen I don't recognize. I think some of them are from our school and some are from the Academy, and I try to figure out which are which based on how they're dressed. It's hard to tell. There are girls and guys, and they all dance in a group around Holden and Gray, like a protective barrier from any Thing-type people who might try to cause trouble. Every time I catch eyes with Holden, he winks and I can see that he has the glow back.

When I slow dance with Ran, I can feel his breath in my ear. It's funny, all these years we've been friends, we've never really been close like this before.

All his familiar smells are stronger so near. I close my eyes and breathe them in.

"Fern," he whispers on our last dance, "I'm really glad you came."

"Me, too," I say. I gently rest my head on his shoulder. He holds me a little closer, as if we are in a slow-dancing hug. I feel happy and sad at the same time. As if our emotions are all mixed up together. I feel his grief, but I feel his happiness, too. Somehow, it makes me feel safe, standing here with my best friend. His arms around me feel like a promise I believe. A promise that despite everything, all will be well after all.

When the song is over, we step away from each other. Ran smiles at me and I smile back, and a million butterflies take flight in my stomach. We find Cassie and head outside. Holden rushes past and yells, "Don't wait up!" over his shoulder as he disappears with Gray and a bunch of his new friends.

"Fag!" I hear someone yell at them from the shadows.

"You know it!" Holden yells, and he and his friends all crack up laughing.

I spot the big headlights of the ice-cream truck turning into the parking lot. "You guys sure you aren't too embarrassed to be seen in the ice-cream truck?" I ask Cassie and Ran.

"Nah," Cassie says. "It's like a really, really big limo."

"With only front seats," Ran adds.

Sara pulls up to the curb, and Ran opens the door. I get in first, then Ran, then Cassie. There aren't enough seat belts, so Ran and I share the middle one.

"Soooo?" Sara asks. "How was it?"

"Great!" we all say at the same time.

We slowly drive through the parking lot and back onto the road. Sara turns up the radio, and we all sing "Crocodile Rock" at the top of our lungs. This is the happiest day of my life, I start to think. But then I stop. Because no happiest day should come after Charlie. But I keep singing, because I know it's OK to be happy at this moment. I know Charlie would want me to be. I can imagine him here now, squeezed in with us, singing and laughing.

Just as we really get into the song, Sara suddenly flicks it off.

"Uh-oh," she says. "Oh … no…" She looks in the rearview mirror. "I can't believe it."

"What?" I ask. But then we all see the flashing lights reflected in the side mirrors.

Sara presses the brakes and pulls to the side of the road.

"Were you speeding?" Ran asks.

"No," Sara says. "Just stay calm. Fern, hand me my purse. Cassie, grab the registration out of the glove compartment."

I give her the purse, and we find the registration.

Sara rolls down her window and squints at the mirror. "Guys, this is our lucky night," she whispers. "Fern, put something over your seat belt, quick!" Ran pulls off his coat and covers our lap just as a cop steps up to the door.

"Mike!" Sara says. "How the heck are ya?"

"Hey, Sara. How's it goin'?"

"You nearly gave me a heart attack. I totally thought we were busted. And I wasn't even speeding! Um, I wasn't, was I?"

"Uh, no, but..."

"Just stopped me to say hi, huh? How've you been, anyway?"

"Uh, Sara? Your dad called you out. He said his truck was stolen."

She laughs but it sounds fake. "Well, it's just us! It's not stolen. So you can call off the search."

"I don't know... ."

"Look, Mike. See these sweet faces?"

We all smile at him. Cassie waves.

"They all just came from Homecoming. Remember how important that was to us when we were in school? And now I have to get them home so they don't get in trouble for missing curfew. You don't want them to remember their first Homecoming as the time when their driver got busted by the police, do you? I mean, *Homecoming memories,* Mike. You know how important they are. Weren't you, like, homecoming king one year?"

"Actually, no. I never went to Homecoming."

Uh-oh.

Sara sighs. "Oh, Mike. Please, for me? Tell you what. You can follow us! You could escort us to Cassie's and Ran's houses, and then I promise to head straight home. You can follow us the whole way. Whatever you want."

I hold my breath. We are in so. Much. Trouble.

Mike taps his fingers on the door.

"Please?" Sara says again.

Please, I say to myself. *Please, please, please, please, please.*

"Oh, what the heck. All right. But don't try anything funny. I'm going to follow you, and I can call for backup if I need it."

"I promise. No funny business. Scout's honor. Or whatever. Thanks, Mike! You're the best cop ever!"

He shakes his head and walks back to his car.

"I can't believe it," Ran says.

"Fern, never say I've never done anything for you, sister."

"Oh. My. God. This is, like, the best night of my life!" Cassie gushes. "I will never forget this night for as long as I live. How cool are we, getting pulled over by the cops! Do you think he'll flash his lights all the way home?"

"Lord, I hope not," Sara says.

"You were good," Ran says. "You totally snowed him."

"Yeah," Sara says, turning the radio back on. "I was pretty awesome."

We drop Cassie off first. She practically skips to her front door. When she gets there, she turns and blows us all kisses. We laugh and blow some back.

At Ran's house, Sara pulls to the curb and parks. The police car is right behind us, but thankfully he parks far enough behind that when he turns off the lights, you can't see him from the house. When Ran gets out, his parents open the front door and come rushing down the front path. His dad has a camera.

"You may as well get out, Fern. There's no way they'll let you guys leave without a pose," Ran says.

I climb out, and his dad gives me a huge hug. Then his mom wraps her long, skinny arms around me and whispers in my ear, "You OK, honey? We've been so worried about you."

I nod my head against her soft sweater. Why is it that when people are nice to you, it makes you have to cry? I squeeze my eyes shut and take a deep breath. She smells like sugar cookies.

"I'm doing OK," I say. She lets me go, and Ran takes my hand and leads me over to the garage door, under the outside light.

"What a beautiful couple," his dad says. Ran squeezes my hand.

Couple?

Ran's dad counts to three and we smile. I don't even blink. "Perfect! I'll have Ran e-mail you a copy. Come on, honey, it's freezing out here." They wave to Sara and rush back inside. The garage light goes out, and suddenly Ran and I are standing in the dark.

"That really was the best night ever," Ran says. He is still holding my hand.

I can't tell him I agree. I feel like ... like there just can't be any *bests* now. Not without Charlie.

"It was really great," I say.

And then Ran's face is up close to mine, and he kisses me so fast, I'm not positive it happened.

"Well, see ya," he says, and rushes up the walk.

"See ya," I whisper, touching my lips with my fingers. But he's too far away to hear.

"Woo-woo!" Sara whistles when I open the door to the truck. "Way to go, Ferny!"

I cringe, but inside I am smiling so big, I think my lips will crack just at the thought.

Sara pulls back onto the road, and we drive home singing to the oldies together. When we turn onto our road, Mike turns on the flashing lights.

"Oh, gimme a break," Sara says. "Is that really necessary?"

I peer through the rearview mirror. "It's pretty funny," I say.

Our dad is standing on the porch with his arms crossed at his chest.

"You ready for this?" Sara asks as we pull into the driveway.

"Bring it."

She laughs. "Fern, you are full of surprises."

"I know," I say. "Who would've thought?"

39

We OPEN OUR DOORS at the same time and step into the cold. Mike has finally turned off the stupid flashing lights.

"Hey, Mr. Wallace. Found your truck-jackers here. You want me to arrest them?"

Boy, he's funny.

"Where's Holden?" my dad asks, ignoring Mike's attempt to lighten the situation.

"Where do you think he is?" Sara asks, handing him the keys to the truck.

Faded Charlie smiles down at us with his giant

ice-cream cone. He really does look like a ghost under that stupid paint job. But his eyes still shine in their happy way. His happiness has always been so catching, but I spent his whole short life trying to avoid it. Maybe I was jealous of not being able to be as happy as he was all the time. Why was I so miserable? I can't remember why. Not now, when I know what real misery is. What real loss and pain are. And I'm not going to let my dad ruin Holden's one happy night. And not mine, either.

"Dad," Sara says. "You've got to get over whatever issue you're having with Holden."

"Don't," he says. "Don't tell me what I have to do. I have a right to worry about my son."

Mike clears his throat. "Uh, well, I'll be going, then, Mr. Wallace. That is, unless you really do want to press charges?"

"No, no, Mike. Thanks. I appreciate you getting them home safely. Stop by the restaurant sometime and I'll give you a meal on the house."

"That won't be necessary," he says. "You girls behave yourselves from now on, all right?"

"Thanks for not arresting us, Mike," Sara says. "Call me!"

It's dark, but I'm sure he's blushing like crazy. "Uh ... sure. OK. Bye." He rushes back to his car and drives away.

When we turn back to my dad, he's standing in front of the truck, looking up at Charlie. His cheeks, wet with tears, sparkle in the outdoor lights shining on us.

"Dad," Sara says quietly, putting a hand on his shoulder, "we didn't mean to upset you. But we did what we thought was right."

He looks so sad, it's hard to be mad at him.

"I know that," he says. "I know you think I'm horrible for talking to Holden like I did. But I ... I just don't think he's ready to be in a relationship. He's just a boy. How can he even know for sure this is what he wants? Who he is?"

"It's who he is for now," I say. "Can't he be who he wants to be now instead of who he's supposed to be in the future? Right now, he's happy. You should have seen him tonight, Dad. He was with all these friends. And he belonged." I picture Holden on the school bus with the Things pinging his ears, and then at the dance with his friends surrounding him in their protective circle. No one is going to ping him ever again.

My dad looks at me as if for the first time.

"My God," he says. "Fern. You're – You look beautiful!"

"Thanks," I say.

"Oh, honey. I'm so sorry. I didn't even ask if you were going. Damn it!" He pounds his fist on the truck just below Charlie's faded face.

I am so used to being overlooked. And usually angry about it. But this time it doesn't bother me. Because it all worked out. It really did. It was so much better to have fun.

"It's OK, Dad. Really."

"No. Nothing is OK." He steps forward and stretches his hands out to support himself against the truck. He looks up and sees that his hands have landed on Charlie's ice-cream cone. He stares at Charlie's sweet face. "Oh, God," he says, and starts to cry harder.

I put my hand on his shoulder. "Dad, it's all right."

"Oh, God," he keeps saying.

I press harder on his shoulder. Charlie smiles at us. He just keeps smiling. Frozen. I want to look away, but I can't. I want to help. But I can't. I don't want to see my dad like this. He's supposed to be the strong one. But now that all of us seem to be ... surviving, he seems like he has let go.

I think about the morning Charlie died. How that strange warmth spread all through me as I lay awake, unable to sleep. I wonder if anyone else felt it. I think part of me died at that moment, too. Maybe part of all of us died. That piece of Charlie that connected us all together unclasped. And now we're all walking around with a missing piece. Maybe my dad's piece is bigger. Maybe it's growing.

"I miss him so much," my dad says, not looking at either of us. "I miss him so much, I don't think I can survive it sometimes."

I look at Sara, fear rising in me. "We know, Dad," she says soothingly. "Let's all go inside."

My dad wipes his eyes and nods. "I wish Holden would get back here," he says.

"Holden is in good hands, Dad. Don't worry."

"He really is," I say. "Promise."

We follow him inside and find my mom in the living room, sipping a glass of wine.

"Where's Holden?" she asks.

"He's with Gray," I say. "He's fine."

"Fern?"

"Yeah, it's me."

My mom puts her glass down and stands up. "Oh, honey. You look beautiful! Where did you get that dress?"

"Cassie's sister."

She puts her hand to her mouth so we can't see it trembling. But then she starts to cry. "I'm so sorry, Fern. I didn't even know you were going."

When she says it, I realize I really should be mad at her. She's my mom. She was supposed to help me get ready. She was supposed to take pictures of me. And Holden.

But I was supposed to tell her I was going in the first place. So what did I expect?

"It's OK, Mom," I say.

"You're so beautiful," she says again, looking at me. I mean really looking at me, and seeing me, as if for the first time in forever.

"Thanks," I say. But I don't think she realizes what for. Or maybe she does.

At around midnight, my parents are starting to freak out. But Sara convinces them to go to bed and promises we'll wake them up when Holden gets home. Sara makes some popcorn and starts to put in a movie. But before it starts, I click PAUSE.

"You know that stuff Dad said?" I ask. "About not knowing if he could survive?"

"Mm-hmmm."

"Do you ever feel that way?"

She puts her arm around me. "Yes, I do. But at the same time, I know I will. I know we all will."

"Mom put his ashes in his bedroom. Did you know that?"

"Yeah."

"I think we should find a better place."

Sara leans her head on my shoulder. "We will. It just takes time."

We stay leaning against each other like that, with her arm around me. It doesn't feel awkward or uncomfortable. It feels familiar.

I wake up on the couch with a start to Holden towering over us. Sara jumps, too.

"Hey," he says, grinning. He twirls in a circle.

"Hey, Cinderella, what time is it?" Sara says.

"One thirty."

"You don't look like a pumpkin to me."

"Cinderella doesn't turn into a pumpkin, you dope. Her carriage does."

"Oh, yeah."

Holden sits down in the oversize chair and kicks off his shoes. He sighs happily.

"Well?" I ask.

"It was good," he says. "Really good."

"Where'd you go after the dance?" Sara asks. "How'd you get home?"

"There was a party at Scott Davies's house. He's a senior at the Academy. We hung out there and watched people get drunk and act stupid. Then this wasted girl threw up on Gray's leg."

"Ew," I say.

"I know. So anyway, we had to wash Gray's pants since we have to return the tuxes tomorrow. We hung out in the laundry room for, like, two hours. And we just talked and stuff. It was really ... nice."

"Just talked," Sara says, grinning. "Right."

"It's true! We decided that we didn't really like each other as boyfriends, and that it was stupid to date each other just because we're the only gay guys we know. So now we're going to try to find boyfriends for each other."

"It's like a real-life fairy tale," Sara says. Then she cracks up. "Fairy. Get it?"

Holden shakes his head. "So not funny."

"Oh, come on," she fake-punches his arm.

"It kind of is," I say.

"Hey, you're supposed to be my trusty sidekick. Don't go over to her side!"

"Fern's no sidekick," Sara says. "She's a free woman."

That makes me feel good. But I'm also glad that Holden still thinks of me that way.

"I'm too hyper to go to bed. Want to take the truck for a spin?" Holden gets up, as if he's seriously ready to go.

"I think Dad swallowed the keys," I say.

"Was it that bad?"

Sara shrugs. "He'll get over it. You know he really is just worried about you."

Holden shakes his head. "You know it's more than that."

"Maybe," she says. "But it's only because he loves you."

"Whatever."

"No," I say. "It's true."

"You've got to cut him some slack. He'll get over it. You know Dad. I think right now he's just hurting so much, he doesn't know how to handle anything."

Holden falls back into the chair. "Do you think we'll ever be OK? I mean, obviously I have these moments where I can feel happy. But then something will remind me of Charlie, and I get so overwhelmed. And Mom..."

We all look toward the stairs.

"She'll get better," Sara says. "It's just going to take time."

She looks over at me. I realize that Sara has been more of a mom to me in the past twenty-four hours – in the past few weeks, even – than my mom has since I can remember. She's been a mom to Holden, too. It seems like she's aged so much so fast. Like she was forced to. It doesn't seem fair.

"Mom will be OK," Sara says. "Dad, too. All of us. It's like the minister said. We all grieve differently. We'll all miss him in our own way."

Her words make me think of my secret, and I know it's not fair to keep it anymore. "There's something I have to show you guys," I say. I hadn't been meaning to tell anyone, but suddenly the moment feels right. "Stay here." I go upstairs and come back down with the answering machine.

"Klepto!" Holden says. "I wondered where that went."

I set it on the coffee table. "I couldn't change the message. I couldn't bear to erase his voice."

Holden reaches out to touch the machine.

"I want to save it," I say. "I know Dad has the 'See You at Harry's' ad on disc somewhere, or we could watch it on YouTube. But this is different. That day I helped Charlie make the message, well, I just remember it so clearly. It was a day I was nice to him."

"You were always nice to him," Sara says.

"No, I wasn't. Anyway, I wanted you to know I have it. In case you ever need to hear him."

"I don't think I could bear listening," Sara says. "But I'm glad you saved it, Fern. Really glad."

"Me, too," Holden says.

We all lean back and watch the answering machine as it sits there on the coffee table. Like it's a treasure that holds a secret only the three of us will ever know. I guess that's exactly what it is.

40

THE FOLLOWING SUNDAY, we all go to the restaurant to help work the Sunday brunch. The restaurant is even more packed than usual. My mom pulls Sara and me aside and reminds us to watch for Silver Purses. This is her code word for the little old ladies who like to put the silverware in their purses. You would be surprised at how many sticky-fingered little old ladies there are in the world. Sometimes they even take the salt and pepper shakers. It's been a family joke forever to come up with the best reason they steal the silverware. Holden's theory is that they take the silverware to their church bazaars to sell and impress the priests. Sara thinks they hoard the utensils, and once they have a set, give them away as wedding gifts to their grandchildren. I think maybe there's some silverware club where there's a contest to see who can gather the most silverware, and you get different points for spoons, knives, and forks. There is a whole underground club throughout the country, and they have these big supersecret conventions where they display their goods. Charlie always liked my theory best. Unfortunately, he believed it. One day he actually caught a lady in the act and marched over to her.

"Mine!" he yelled. Then he reached into her purse and pulled out a fork.

The poor lady looked like she was going to have a heart attack. "I don't know how that got in there!" she kept saying in a shaky voice. The other old ladies she was sitting with looked horrified, but we all thought they probably had a spoon or two in their own purses.

My mom gives us each a quick hug before she rushes off to help Mona wait tables. Sara smiles at me as we watch my mom greet customers in her old, happy voice. It's a start.

"Hey, Fern!" Holden says in a loud whisper, coming up to me with a rubber bin for dirty dishes. "Check out those three guys over there. Do you know them?"

I look to where he's gesturing. There are three cute boys at a booth. They look about college age. What is it with Holden and older men?

"No," I say.

"What do you think?"

"They're kind of good-looking, I guess. But they're too old for you."

"Noooo. You know. What do you *think*?"

"I thought this was Gray's job. To help you. I don't know how to tell."

He rolls his eyes. "You're useless. Go wait on them and see if you can figure it out."

"I'm not a waitress!"

"Oh, forget it. I'll ask Sara."

"No! Wait. I'll do it." Holden actually kisses me on the cheek.

I like the new Holden. In fact, I love him. Well, yes. Obviously. I always have.

I grab a pad and start to walk over to the boys. But my mom beats me to them. I turn back and Holden shrugs.

"Useless," he mouths.

The morning flies by. At two o'clock the last customers finally waddle out, and Sara flips the OPEN sign to CLOSED. Then all the staff get together to eat leftovers just like old times. Except for one thing.

And yet he is here. I can feel his warmth. I can feel how he's brought us together. It's as if before Charlie died, my family was connected in a circle, as if we were holding hands. But when he died, we let go. Now, somehow, Charlie has helped us link hands again. Sitting at the table, I can feel Charlie here as if he never left. He is here, just in a different way. I can feel him under the table, threatening to try to tie my shoes to Holden's. He's here next to me, saying how much Doll loves their sundae. He's here reaching for my hand, whispering in my ear. *I love you, Ferny.*

See you at Hawee's, I hear him say. And it doesn't feel like a lie anymore.

He is here. And he is not here. He is love. That's what's left. I think again of the poem the minister read at Charlie's service. I still have it in my jewelry box. I haven't read it yet. I can't. But I remember one line the minister read: *When all that's left of me is love, give me away.* And I finally understand how to do that. I reach for Holden's hand on one side of me and Sara's on the other. I give them each a quick squeeze, then start to let go. But at the same time, they both squeeze back. "It means I love you," my mother taught us. "It's how you say it when you don't want anyone else to hear."

So I squeeze one more time. This time for Charlie. I am giving him away, and I am getting him back in the way Charlie knew best to give. And it is enough.

Acknowledgments

"Thank you" is such a tiny phrase for such a big gesture. I wish I could think of something more grandiose and appropriate to convey how truly grateful I am to the people who made this book possible. To my agent, Barry Goldblatt, for telling me, "Someday you need to write about growing up in the restaurant business" – and for waiting ten years for me to do it. To my editor, Joan Powers, for guiding me through the thicket and brambles, as she always does, with kindness and patience. To Holly Black, for our hours-long talk that saved this book. To Robin Wasserman and Libba Bray, for saying just the right things at just the right time, as usual. To my writing partners, Cindy Faughnan and Debbi Michiko Florence, for reading multiple drafts and keeping my spirits up whenever I thought it was just too hard. To my son, Eli, for saying those magic words every writer longs to hear: "Keep reading." And to my husband, Peter, for reading and listening and cheering me on through it all. Thank you.

THE SKY IS EVERYWHERE
JANDY NELSON

What kind of girl wants to kiss every boy at
a funeral, wants to maul a guy in a tree after
making out with her (dead) sister's boyfriend the
previous night? Speaking of which, what kind of
girl makes out with her sister's boyfriend, at all?

"The book of the year... this book is
perfection." *Carly Bennet* (blogger)

"Heartwarming." *Independent*

COLD HANDS, WARM HEART
JILL WOLFSON

Dani was born with a heart of the wrong side of her body. In her fifteen years of life, she's had more doctors' appointments, X-rays and tests – eaten more green hospital jelly – than she cares to think about. Fourteen–year-old Amanda is a competitive gymnast, her body a small package of sleek muscles, in perfect health.

The two girls don't know each other, don't go to the same school and don't have any friends in common.

But their lives are about to collide.

WAFFLE HEARTS
MARIA PARR

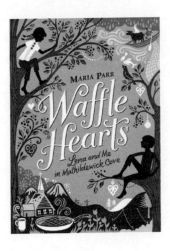

Whether it's putting a cow in a boat or advertising for a dad, no day is ordinary with a best friend like Lena.

Trille loves to share everything with her, even Auntie Granny's waffles. But when Lena faces a secret she can't share, will their friendship end?

SURFACING
NORA RALEIGH BASKIN

School swim-team star Maggie Paris has
an uncanny, almost magical ability to draw
out people's deepest truths, even when they
don't intend to share them. Her classmates
are avoiding her and even her parents, busy
at avoiding each other, have become wary,
not wanting to confront the secret deep
at the heart of their devastated family.

A lyrical and deeply moving story
about finding the courage to confront
your ghosts – one truth at a time.

Jo Knowles is the author of *Jumping Off Swings*, which, in a starred review, *Publishers Weekly* called "absorbing from first page to last," and *Lessons from a Dead Girl*, which *Kirkus Reviews* described as "a razor-sharp examination of friendship, abuse, and secrets."

About this new novel, she says, "Some years ago, my agent suggested that I write a book reflecting my own experience growing up in the restaurant business. When I began, I imagined the book as a gift to my brother, in which I could rewrite our past and make it kinder and more gentle. But I soon realized that these characters weren't us and that fate had other plans for them. Ironically, by writing this story about strangers whom I came to love, I was able to understand my own family story more clearly." Jo Knowles lives in Vermont, USA.